Paws & Pastries

Also by BARBARA HINSKE
The Rosemont Series
Coming to Rosemont
Weaving the Strands
Uncovering Secrets
Drawing Close
Bringing Them Home
Shelving Doubts
Restoring What Was Lost

Novellas
The Night Train
The Christmas Club (adapted for The Hallmark Channel, 2019)

Novels in the Emily Series
Guiding Emily

Novels in the "Who's There?!" Collection
DEADLY PARCEL
FINAL CIRCUIT

Connect with BARBARA HINSKE Online
Sign up for her newsletter at **BarbaraHinske.com** to receive a Free Gift, plus Inside Scoops and Bedtime Stories.

Search for **Barbara Hinske on YouTub**e to tour inside her historic home, plus learn tips and tricks for busy women!

Find photos of fictional Rosemont and Westbury, adorable dogs, and things related to her books at **Pinterest.com/BarbaraHinske**.

Facebook.com/BHinske
Twitter.com/BarbaraHinske
Instagram/barbarahinskeauthor
bhinske@gmail.com

Paws & Pastries

BARBARA HINSKE

Casa del Northern Publishing
Phoenix, Arizona

ISBN: 978-1-7349249-2-3
Library of Congress Control Number: 2020920470

Casa del Northern Publishing
Phoenix, Arizona

Dedication

To my mother, Harriett Hinske, and my grandmother, Pauline Stahler, for making the holidays magical and sharing their love of baking.

Chapter 1

Clara Conway loosened her grip on the steering wheel and relaxed into the driver's seat. The illuminated highway sign indicated that hers was the next exit. Two more miles—she was almost home.

She'd been fighting to stay awake for the last hundred miles or so, the rhythmic *swish-swish* of her windshield wipers nearly lulling her to sleep. Shortly after four this afternoon—when she was pulling away from her mother's house for what she knew would be the last time—she'd already felt exhausted. She expected she'd be home by one—one thirty at the latest. What she didn't expect was the freezing rain that started as soon as it grew dark. The trees that had been an explosion of color on her drive to her mother's, were now barren and skeletal. The cheerless weather of late autumn in the Midwest had arrived. She'd be lucky if she got home in one piece.

The sign overhead announced her exit. Clara squinted at the clock on the dashboard. Three fifteen. Had she ever driven this many hours without stopping? She looked over her right shoulder. She needed to merge into the exit lane for her own neighborhood—she was far too tired to keep driving down to *her* street.

Travis had assured her that his affair with his dental hygienist was over. He'd sworn Melanie had been a "big mistake" and that he'd let her go as soon as he hired her replacement. Clara had nothing to worry about, he said, she could go to her mother's bedside in the ICU and be "fully present" there.

Clara glanced up at the sign for her exit as she sailed past in the left lane. Her husband said all the right things—offered all of the appropriate platitudes—but trust wasn't rebuilt with words. It required action. She'd caught Travis in a lie too many times.

Melanie lived in a modest bungalow, two streets off the next exit. Clara knew it well. She'd seen her husband's car parked at the curb numerous times in the past year.

Driving by Melanie's house on the way home had become a mindless routine. Her car instinctively knew the way and floated toward the exit.

Her steering wheel suddenly lurched right, and Clara's back went rigid. The car was fishtailing down the exit ramp. She twisted the wheel hard to the left, pressed her foot firmly on the anti-lock brakes, and managed to regain control of the vehicle before reaching the intersection at the end of the ramp.

She was out of her mind to be doing a drive-by on a night like this. She lowered her driver's side window a crack and inhaled the freezing air. She shuddered and blinked rapidly, suddenly feeling fully alert.

Clara steered the car slowly into a right turn, then inched forward on the residential street that was covered in thick gray frozen tire-track slush. She was careful to avoid sliding into one of the parked cars that lined either side. The moon was cordoned off by thick clouds. Clara's headlights provided the only illumination in the darkness that shrouded the street.

She sucked in another deep breath. The cars parked along the road were all coated in a thin layer of ice. She leaned forward, hunched over the steering wheel.

There could be no mistake, even from fifty yards back. Travis's two-seater Mercedes convertible stuck out in this neighborhood like a sore thumb. That car—and the man who owned it—didn't belong here—*on this street*—in the middle of the night.

The tears she hadn't yet shed for her mother welled up in Clara's eyes and stung as they traveled down her frigid cheeks, splashing onto the steering column. She turned her head as she pulled alongside the familiar car.

Her fears were confirmed. Her husband was, once more, spending the night with Melanie. Had he ever broken off the affair, as he'd promised? Clara mopped her face with a gloved hand. She didn't think so. Her husband was a liar and a cheater. That fact would never change.

She wanted to get off this street as fast as possible; she hit the gas, but her front tire hit a thick rut in the ice, jerking the steering wheel out of her hands. She grabbed at it to regain control, but was too late. The front bumper of her car screeched along the side of his precious car. Clara squeezed her eyes shut and pumped the brake until her car came to a complete stop.

The street was deadly silent. She rolled down the passenger window and leaned over, looking back at the path she'd just traced.

A linear dent creased the side of Travis's car, from the rear wheel to the end of the driver's side door. The side mirror swung limply, suspended from its wires.

She turned to the street in front of her and powered the windows up. Travis would be livid. He'd probably try to cajole her into making the insurance claim, arranging for a rental car, and scheduling the repairs. Under the circumstances, he wouldn't dare suggest she caused the damage, even if he noticed his paint on her bumper. A slow smile crept across her face. She put the car in gear and made her way safely home.

Clara slipped her car into her spot in the two-car garage, turned off the ignition, and pressed the button to close the door. The stress of the long, dangerous drive coupled with the emotional toll of her mother's unexpected death and her husband's exceptional infidelity, pressed down on her shoulders like a hundred-pound weight.

She hoisted herself out of the driver's seat and made a beeline for the door into the house. Unloading the few family heirlooms and scant remains of her mother's possessions would have to wait until morning. She hadn't told Travis that she was driving home a day earlier than planned—she'd meant it to be a nice surprise. It looked like the surprise was on her. With any luck, he'd go straight to his dental practice from Melanie's, without stopping at home.

She didn't have the energy to deal with Travis. Her mother's stroke, and unexpected death on the day she was supposed to be released from the hospital, had left Clara raw and empty.

She made her way into the master bedroom and kicked off her boots, flipping on the overhead light. She froze when she saw the bed. It was neatly made, every decorative pillow properly aligned and in place—just the way she'd left it when she'd gone to her mother, ten days ago. Travis had never made a bed in his life. She felt hot tears at the back of her throat. Travis hadn't spent a night at home since she'd left.

Clara turned on her heel and moved noiselessly down the hall to the guest room. The last person to sleep in that bed had been her mother—not more than six months ago. She'd come for a long weekend to celebrate Clara's birthday—before the stroke had taken her life.

Clara pulled back the covers and slipped into bed, too tired to even take off her clothes. She buried her nose in the pillow, her thick mane of chestnut hair cocooning her face. She inhaled deeply and thought she caught a trace of her mother's scent. It couldn't be, she told herself. She'd washed the sheets after her mother's visit. Still, the sensation was comforting, and she stretched her legs to the ends of her toes. Exhaustion laid its claim on her. She'd figure out what to do about her life when she woke up.

Brittle sunshine broke through the icy window in jagged tentacles across the foot of the bed and onto the floor. Clara cracked one eye open and groaned. She hadn't bothered to close the drapes when she'd stumbled into bed, and now—at half-past nine—sun poured through the east-facing window.

She propped herself on her elbow and noticed that her pillowcase was soggy. She pushed damp tendrils of hair off of her forehead. She must have been crying in her sleep. Again.

Clara thought about closing the drapes and crawling back into bed but quickly discarded the idea. The image of Travis's car from last night—and all that it signified—together with a throbbing headache would not let her go back to sleep.

She forced herself out of bed and headed for the master bathroom. She splashed water on her face and took two Ibuprofen. She'd make herself a pot of coffee. By the time she finished her first cup, she'd be feeling human again.

Clara removed the pot from the coffeemaker and inserted her tall cup under the stream of dark brown liquid until it was almost full, switching containers with a practiced motion so that no liquid spilled onto the counter. She cradled the cup with both hands, the hot ceramic almost painful to the touch.

She padded around her house in her socks, looking at the furniture and decor as if she'd never seen them before—as if she were evaluating the lives of people she'd never met before.

With the exception of the carved cuckoo clock in the living room—a wedding gift from her Swiss grandfather—and a set of dishes she'd purchased at an auction with her first paycheck that were displayed in the china cabinet, nothing in the house held any resonance for her. It all reflected Travis's taste and personal preferences.

She returned to the kitchen and took a sip of her coffee. Less than twenty-four hours ago, she'd been seated in the office of her mother's lawyer. An only child of an only child, Clara and her mom had always been close. Their shared love of baking was a passion that had brought them great joy over the years. One of Clara's earliest memories was standing on a stool next to her mother, mixing cake batter and rolling out cookie dough on the worn butcher block countertop. As Clara got older, the recipes had become more complicated and more delicious. Baking was their special time together. Now, tucked safely in the trunk of her car, was a box of her mother's baking pans, her special rolling pin, and the metal cookie cutters from Clara's childhood.

Clara had been the sole person mentioned in the will. She'd known that would be the case. Her parents had divorced when Clara was a toddler and her father had died of cancer soon after. It had always been just Clara and her mother. What she hadn't known was that her mother's frugal ways were not a reflection of her means: Clara's mother had been careful with her money all of her life and had invested it well. For a woman who didn't know how to use a smartphone, her mother had acquired an impressive portfolio of stocks in Apple and other technology leaders. Clara had left the lawyer's office with a sizable nest egg and a handwritten letter from her mother, directing her to spend it in ways and on things that would make Clara's dreams come true.

She'd known immediately what her mom had meant. She'd packed everything of her mother's that she'd wanted to save into her car, turned the keys over to the local realtor who was going to supervise the sale of her mother's tiny house and her remaining possessions, and headed for home. And Travis.

She was beyond excited to share her news. Thanks to her inheritance, she now had more than enough money to open the patisserie that she'd wanted to run since she'd visited one on a high school trip to France years ago. She would quit her job as a hospital dietician and open a bakery. She wouldn't need any money from him, and her inheritance would allow her to contribute her share of their joint expenses, without having to rely on her salary. Travis had thrown cold water on her dream the entire ten years they'd been married, but he could have no objection to her making it a reality, now.

She drained her cup and poured another. As usual, Travis always managed to take the wind out of her sails. She was bringing the cup to her lips when she heard her mother's voice in her head. *What has Travis got to do with this? This is your money and your life. Don't let him control you. Take charge. Go after your dream.*

Clara set the mug on the counter and looked around. She didn't believe that people talked to you from the other side, but it certainly sounded like her mother. She straightened, and the air around her prickled with electricity. She would follow this inner voice—whether it was her intuition or her mother from beyond.

Clara dumped the rest of the coffee down the sink and turned off the pot. She flipped open the kitchen cupboards and drawers, removing the utensils, knives, and gadgets that were her favorites. She retrieved a roll of trash bags from the pantry and bagged the items.

She then moved into the master bedroom and quickly stashed her clothes and shoes into trash bags. Her makeup and toiletries came next.

She knew that these items, when added to the things already loaded into her car from the day before, would leave scant room for anything else. She carried everything to her small SUV and spent fifteen minutes shifting things around and reloading the car to make maximum use of the available space.

When she was finished, she stepped back and assessed what she had done. She smiled and nodded slowly. She'd have just enough room for the clock and her beloved dishes. She grabbed a stack of old newspapers from the garage and completed packing.

A little more than two hours later, with every conceivable space in the SUV pressed into service, she was done. She had the things she wanted to take into her new life.

She opened her laptop and typed an email to her supervisor at the hospital. She informed him that she would not be returning from the FMLA leave that she'd taken to care for her mother and thanked the hospital for the opportunity to work there. In truth, her boss had been consistently obnoxious and overbearing, and downright nasty when she'd informed him she needed to take time off to care for her mother. She wouldn't miss that job—or her employer—one little bit.

All that remained was to leave a note for Travis. She dug a piece of paper and a pen out of a drawer.

She paused, her hand hovering over the paper. What would she say? Pouring her heart out—venting her years of anger, hurt, and frustration—would take hours. *Will he care about how I feel? Has he ever cared?*

Now that she was packed and ready to go, Clara was anxious to get away—before she lost her nerve. She wanted to start this new life that she would craft for herself. Alone—all alone. She wouldn't allow a man to hold her back or keep her down ever again.

Clara folded the paper in half and scribbled I'M DONE in bold capitals across the page. She tented the paper on the kitchen counter, pulled the house key off of her key ring, and set it next to the paper.

Clara walked through the house a final time. Satisfied that she was ready, she backed her SUV out of the garage, closed the door, and deposited the garage door opener in their mailbox.

Ten minutes later, she approached the major interstate highway that crossed her state from east to west. She noted the overhead signs indicating the appropriate lane to be in. Everything she knew, everything that was familiar—her mother's house, her college, the hospital where she'd held her first position as a dietician (and where she'd met Travis)—was to the east.

Clara took a deep breath and got into the lane to enter the freeway, heading west.

Chapter 2

Clara kept her car radio tuned to whatever country music station she could get reception for as the miles piled up, separating her from her former life. The raw emotion of the he-done-me-wrong songs and the resilience of those focused on fresh starts acted as a balm to her tattered soul.

She stopped for gas and a trip to the restroom as the sun was beginning to set. She picked up a soda and a large bag of trail mix—the kind with M&M's, her very favorite—from the small convenience store at the gas station. She opened the bag and was eating a small handful of the mixture before she got back on the road when her phone pinged with a text message.

Clara hesitated and took a swig of her soda before pulling the phone out of her purse. She tapped the screen and her eyes widened as she read the message from Travis.

> *You must be home by now. I have to work late. Emergency repair of a broken crown. Go ahead and eat without me. Sorry. Don't wait up.*

He didn't know that she had left him—that her days of waiting for him were permanently over. He was undoubtedly spending the evening with Melanie—on the day that his wife was supposed to come home after burying her mother. Bile rose in her throat and she swallowed hard to force it down. Travis Conway was a selfish, heartless excuse of a man.

Feeling revived by the short break and vindicated by Travis's text, Clara pulled back onto the highway and resumed her journey toward her dreams.

Her headlights cut through vast swaths of farmland, punctuated every twenty miles or so by small towns whose existence was announced by a single freeway sign—or at most, two. She was passing through a hilly stretch, the outlines of tall trees—predominantly pines—standing sentry on either side of the highway, when her check engine light came on.

Clara blinked hard and stared at the dashboard. She wasn't imagining things—the check engine light glowed bright and steady. She grimaced. She didn't know much about cars, but she knew that this indicator light meant business. It couldn't be ignored. She was considering pulling onto the shoulder when a sign on her right announced that Pinewood was accessible from the next three exits. Clara didn't want to be stranded on the side of the road after dark, so she decided to push on to the first exit for Pinewood.

She glanced nervously from the highway to the instrument cluster on her dashboard as she covered the three miles to the exit. Her car behaved normally, and steam didn't appear from under her hood.

She pulled off the highway and released the breath she had been holding when she saw the tall, illuminated sign of a garage on her right, at the end of the exit ramp.

Andy's Automotive was housed in a tidy red brick building. Square planters holding neatly trimmed evergreens flanked the glass entry. A sign that read *Open to Serve You* hung from a wire on the door. She pulled in and drove past the gas pumps to a parking area across from a row of service bays. All except one of the bays were dark.

She relaxed her death grip on the steering wheel, got out of the car, and headed toward the lighted service bay.

"Hello?" she called. The cab of an eighteen-wheeler stood in the middle of the lot with one side of its engine exposed. "Anybody here?"

An older man in coveralls stepped around the front of the truck and came into view, wiping his hands on an oily rag.

"Hello, miss," he said. His tone was congenial but the dark circles under his brown eyes telegraphed fatigue. "Can I help you?"

"Thank God," she said, bringing her hand to her heart. "Yes. I was on the highway and my check engine light came on. Scared me to death," she said, continuing in a rush. "I know that's something you can't ignore so I got off at the first exit, hoping to find someone who can fix it for me."

He leaned against the truck and regarded her thoughtfully. When he spoke, his voice was warm and reassuring. "That was very smart of you. Ignoring that warning light can be a direct route to needing a new engine. Not something anybody wants."

"Can you fix it?" she asked, turning to point to her car.

"I'm sure we can help you," he said. "We'll look at it first thing in the morning."

Her shoulders sagged. "Can't you look at it now?"

He shook his head. "I've been here since before seven this morning, and I'll be back that early tomorrow. I was just getting ready to turn out the lights when you came in."

Tears pricked the backs of her eyes. Here she was—broken down in the middle of nowhere—with no place to stay and no way to get there, even if she had. She sniffled loudly and fumbled in her purse for a tissue.

The man reached into his pocket and withdrew a business card. "Andy Rodriquez," he said, handing it to her. "This is my garage. I've been in business here for almost forty years. Are you from around here?"

Clara shook her head and took a breath to collect herself. "I'll need a place to stay tonight. Any recommendations?"

"The Pinewood Springs Motel, half a mile up the road. It's clean and safe. Johanson's Diner, next to the motel, has the best food in town."

Clara blew her nose and gave him a bleary-eyed smile. "Do you think they'll have a vacancy?"

"On a Thursday night? I'm sure they will. How about I give you a lift over there. It's on my way home."

She hesitated. This Andy Rodriquez was a complete stranger to her.

"I'm sorry, but we don't have taxis or ride shares in Pinewood. It's either ride with me or walk there."

She ran her eyes over his face and shook her head. She wasn't getting into a car with a stranger. "Half a mile up the road, you say?"

He pointed over his shoulder. "Yep. A straight shot. You can't miss it."

"Thank you," she said.

"Do you want to leave your car key with me?" he asked. "I can look at it first thing and give you a call?"

"Good idea. Let me get my bag out of the car and I'll bring the key to you."

Andy nodded his agreement. He shut the door to the bay and watched as she wrestled a rolling suitcase from her loaded-down car.

She set off toward him, her suitcase bumping across the uneven asphalt.

He met her halfway. "Are you sure you want to wrangle that suitcase the half mile to the motel?"

"I'll be fine," she replied, a bit breathless from effort. She handed him her key and a slip of paper with her name and phone number.

"Welcome to Pinewood, Miss Conway," Andy said. "I can see that you're a self-sufficient young woman, but I'm an old-fashioned guy, so I hope you don't mind that I'm going to follow along behind you in my car."

"That's ridiculous," she began, but he held up a hand to stop her.

"It's late, it's dark, and I'm not going to come in tomorrow to learn that my newest customer spent the night in a ditch with a broken ankle."

"That's completely unnecessary."

"That may be, but I'm going to do it anyway."

She shook her head and turned, walking in the direction of the motel.

"If you change your mind along the way and would like a lift, just wave to me. My offer still stands."

Clara set out along the shoulder of the road, marching toward the neon sign in the distance. *Pinewood Springs Motel* glowed in yellow neon script and was outlined by a green neon flourish, with a blue neon river flowing along the bottom. At another time in her life she might have thought it kitschy and tacky, but right now it was the most welcome sight in the world.

Andy, true to his word, crept along the road slightly behind her, his headlights helpfully illuminating the path in front of her.

Pebbles lodged themselves in the wheels of her suitcase twice, but both times she was able to dislodge them by bumping her suitcase onto the pavement. Twenty minutes after she'd left the garage, she had the key to her motel room in her hand.

She stepped out of the office to find that Andy had waited, idling in the parking lot. She held up her key and gestured to him with a thumbs up sign.

Andy flashed his lights in answer, and she watched as he pulled onto the road. Once more, tears stung her eyes. It was very kind of him to see her safely to the motel. Maybe there *were* still some decent men out there.

She looked at the diner on the other side of the motel parking lot. A closed sign shone in the window. She was glad she'd thought to grab the bag of trail mix. A wave of fatigue washed over her, and she began the short trek to her room. With any luck, she'd be asleep in no time.

Chapter 3

Clara woke to a gnawing hunger the next morning. She reached for the bag of trail mix that she'd left open on the nightstand and scooped the last few crumbs into her mouth. The bedside clock told her that it was almost ten-thirty. She hadn't eaten a decent meal since before she'd left her mother's house and had slept in the same clothes for the second night running. She needed to get hold of herself.

Clara threw back the thick down duvet that had been so warm and cozy when she'd crawled into bed the night before and settled her feet into the plush carpet. She went to the window and parted the flowered curtains to allow a sliver of daylight into the room. The walls were painted a buttery yellow. An armchair was upholstered in fabric that matched the drapes. The duvet and bed linens were crisp white. A triple dresser and nightstand of polished mahogany completed the furnishings. The décor might be a bit dated, but it was attractive and welcoming.

Clara felt her shoulders relax as she headed for the bathroom. She turned on the spigot for the shower and was pleasantly surprised to find travel-sized bottles of shampoo and conditioner waiting for her. The hot water was plentiful. She lingered in the steady stream of the shower, allowing the water to wash away her fear and anxiety.

She towel-dried her hair and applied lipstick and blush from her purse. She'd left the rest of her makeup and toiletries in her car.

She picked up her phone, scrolling for a message from Andy about her car. There was nothing from him, but her readout showed five missed calls and ten text messages from Travis. She was glad she'd put her phone on silent when she'd gotten into bed. She'd needed a good night's sleep, not a fight with Travis. In fact, she never needed to fight with Travis again.

Clara googled the only attorney she'd known in what she now thought of as her old hometown. He'd been married to one of her coworkers at the hospital and specialized in family law. It was time to get the ball rolling on her divorce.

Her call to the attorney lasted no more than thirty minutes. He'd tried to talk her out of her plan to relinquish most of their joint assets to her husband, but she'd been insistent. She knew that Travis would try to use all of their stuff as a bargaining chip to prolong the process of finalizing their divorce. He'd be more angered and humiliated that *she* had dumped him, that *she* had been the one to file for divorce, than he would be upset about the divorce itself.

Clara hung up with the understanding that the attorney would file the papers and serve them on Travis a week from the following Wednesday. Thanksgiving was next week, and her attorney was going out of town. She hated the idea of waiting, but a few more days wouldn't matter. The attorney would email her forms that she could sign electronically, and he'd get started.

It was now almost noon and the hollow ache in her stomach demanded her attention.

She dragged the purse-sized brush through her hair and pulled it into a high ponytail that still extended past her shoulders. Clara slipped into a clean sweater and jeans and checked her reflection in the mirror. The bags under her eyes were still there but starting to fade. She saw the reflection of a broken woman, with a bruised and battered heart, but she didn't think anyone else would see that.

She snatched up her phone, and her fingers hovered over the screen. She should listen to her messages and read her texts.

Clara rested the phone against her chin and inhaled slowly. There wouldn't be any surprises in Travis's communications to her. Whatever he had to say could wait. She was hungry.

She took her phone off silent mode, stashing it in her purse. She shoved her feet into her boots, grabbed her coat, and headed to the diner.

Cars jammed the parking lot and two more pulled up as she approached. The food must be as good as Andy had said, judging by the lunchtime crowd.

Clara pulled open the heavy wooden door with beveled glass panes on the top half. The air was moist and fragrant with the aroma of strong coffee and bacon. A sign on the wall in front of her declared: *Breakfast Happily Served All Day—It's the Most Important Meal of the Day*. Booths with shiny red vinyl seats lined the exterior walls. A Formica-topped lunch counter swept along one side of the dining room. Chrome bar stools, upholstered in the same shiny red vinyl, were affixed to the floor in front of the counter. She felt like she had stepped back in time—like she was on the set of the old television series *Happy Days*.

Someone inserted coins in the jukebox and the unmistakable sound of Hank Williams singing "Your Cheatin' Heart" rang out.

She smiled at the irony of the song choice. She scanned the room, looking for the hostess. A short, stocky man with warm brown eyes and a shock of white hair shuttled spryly back and forth behind the lunch counter. He caught her eye and told her to sit wherever she could find a spot.

Clara made her way around the restaurant and seized an open stool at the lunch counter as the person occupying it got up to leave. A coffee cup sat, face down, on a square paper napkin in front of her. She'd no sooner turned it over than the small man leaned over and filled her cup. He nodded to an old-style chrome-and-glass sugar dispenser and a bowl of individual containers of creamer that sat in front of the person next to her.

She shook her head and mouthed the word, "Black."

"I'll be right with you," he said, placing a menu shielded in clear plastic in front of her.

Clara opened the trifold menu and looked over her options. In addition to traditional diner fare, they offered a selection of innovative bruschetta, a grilled vegetable board, and an impressive list of fresh fish. The assortment of pies and cakes on the back page—all homemade—took her breath away. Could a place like this really turn out a Génoise sponge iced with buttercream and finished with a mirror glaze? It was listed as the featured dessert on Fridays. She would have to find out.

She ordered something called a meat lover's skillet, with two eggs over easy, a side of sourdough toast, and a slice of the featured cake.

"Good idea," the man said, smiling at her. "I'm usually sold out before lunch is over."

"This is an extremely interesting menu," she said after he brought the skillet out and she'd taken the first few delicious bites.

"Thank you. My wife's the creative genius behind all of that."

"I'd love to meet her," Clara said, "and give her my compliments on this delicious dish."

The smile never left his lips, but the lines around his eyes tightened. "She wasn't well enough to come in today."

"I'm sorry to hear that," Clara said

"She had a stroke six months ago and isn't back to the restaurant full time. We really miss her around here. It's impossible to find anyone who can cook to her standards—let alone bake like she can. She felt good yesterday and made the cake that you'll taste when you've finished that skillet. Some days, we simply can't supply everything on our menu."

"I'm so sorry," Clara reiterated. "Please be sure to pass along my compliments to her. I hope she continues to recover."

The man nodded and moved to the other end of the counter.

Clara tucked into her meal and relished every bite. She told herself she should stop eating—that she needed to save room for the slice of cake she'd ordered. If it was as good as what she'd just had, she knew she'd want to polish off every crumb. She hadn't eaten much the day before, she rationalized. She was simply catching up.

The man on the stool next to her set his payment on the counter and stepped away.

No sooner had his place been wiped clean and a new mug set than a tall, dark-haired man around Clara's age, with rugged not-quite-handsome features, dressed in a crisp white shirt, dark gray suit, and red-and-gray striped tie, slipped onto the vacant stool.

"Afternoon, Josef," the man now sitting next to her said.

"Hey, Kurt," Josef said from behind the counter, setting a beautiful slice of cake in front of Clara and filling Kurt's overturned mug. "The usual?" He turned to the kitchen to place the order, not waiting for Kurt's reply.

Josef topped off Clara's coffee as she sank her fork into the airy sponge and fluffy buttercream topped with the shiny mirror glaze. She brought the fork to her lips and groaned when she tasted the first bite.

"Good, isn't it?" Josef smiled. "Maisie hasn't lost her touch."

Clara covered her mouth with her hand. "She most certainly hasn't. This is divine." She took a sip of her coffee.

"Let me introduce myself." He extended his hand to her, over the counter. "I'm Josef Johanson. My wife, Maisie, and I have owned this diner for more than forty years."

"Nice to meet you," Clara said. "I'm Clara Conway and I'm extremely impressed." She tapped the menu.

"Then you'll have to come back. Do you live around here?"

She shook her head. "I was waylaid here by car troubles. My car's being looked at by Andy, at the garage down the street. He's the one who recommended your diner."

"He's a good man. You're in capable hands. He's honest and knows how to fix anything."

"That's reassuring to hear."

"When will you be on your way?"

"I don't know. I haven't heard from him yet, about what's wrong with it. My check engine light was on."

"Ohhh … that can be serious. You might be stuck here for a while. If you are, please come back to see us."

"If I am, I'm afraid you'll be seeing me for every meal. You're walking distance from where I'm staying."

Josef looked from Clara to the man in the gray suit, who'd been scrolling through and responding to messages on his phone. Josef's eyes twinkled. "Let me introduce the two of you," he said. He leaned over and touched the younger man's elbow.

"Clara, I'd like you to meet Kurt Holbrook, Pinewood's favorite lawyer."

Kurt extended his hand. "Nice to meet you," he said stiffly.

"Clara may be spending a few days with us," Josef said. "It might be nice if someone showed her the sights."

"No, really ..." Clara stammered. "I'm fine on my own."

"I'll be working on motions all weekend," Kurt replied.

Josef pursed his lips and narrowed his eyes at Kurt.

"I hope you enjoy your stay here," Kurt added before returning his attention to his cell phone.

"With any luck, I'll be on my way after lunch." Her phone began to ring in her purse. "That's probably the repair shop, now," she said to Josef. "Would you mind boxing up the rest of this piece of cake to go? I plan to eat every last crumb."

Chapter 4

"I've got good news and bad news," Andy said.

Clara exited the diner and stepped to one side. She cradled her phone between her cheek and her shoulder as she zipped her jacket against the chill.

"Are you there?" Andy asked.

"Yes. Sorry. Please—just tell me."

"You need a new alternator. Your battery needs to be replaced, too."

She blew out a breath. "That's good, right? My engine is fine?"

"Your engine is perfectly fine. I performed a quick diagnostic on the rest of your SUV—wouldn't want you breaking down on the highway again—and everything else is in great shape. It's obvious you've maintained your car."

"How much will a new alternator and battery cost?"

"On your car, they'll run just under a thousand dollars."

"I can afford that. Is that the bad news?"

"Not exactly. Because you have a Porsche SUV, I can't find the part you need anywhere within three hundred miles. That's why it's taken me so long to get back to you. I've been calling around, looking for that alternator. I know that you're on your way somewhere—I'm assuming for Thanksgiving next week—but I won't have the part until the middle of the week after Thanksgiving."

Clara sucked in a breath.

"An overnight courier might get it here the Monday after Thanksgiving—for an additional two hundred dollars. I'm sorry that I can't get you on your way any sooner than that. I'll help you arrange a rental car, if you'd like."

Clara turned her face into the stiff breeze and brushed back the tendrils that had worked themselves loose from her ponytail. "It's fine. I wasn't headed anywhere in particular, and I don't have plans for Thanksgiving. I'll wait here until it's fixed."

"I'll order the part as soon as we hang up, and I'll install it the minute it arrives." He paused, then continued. "Are you comfortable at the Pinewood Springs Motel?"

"Yes. And the diner you recommended is a treasure. I've just eaten the most glorious piece of cake I've had in years. I can think of far worse places to spend the next ten days."

"Good," Andy said. "I'm happy that you're comfortable."

Clara was touched by his concern. "Don't worry about me. Do you mind if I stop by, now, to get some things out of my car?"

"That'll be fine. It looks like you've got all of your worldly possessions in your car."

Clara paused. "I guess I do," she finally replied.

"I'll keep it locked up in one of the bays until the part comes. We don't want anyone breaking into it in the parking lot."

"Thank you. That's very kind of you. I'll see you in about fifteen minutes. I'm walking over from the diner."

"When you're done getting your things, I'll be more than happy to drive you back to your motel."

"Thank you, but I'm sure I can manage on my own."

Clara disconnected the call and began walking, the gravel of the parking lot making a satisfying crunch under her heels. She paused before stepping onto the shoulder of the road. She really should retrieve Travis's messages.

Clara tapped on the screen, brought her phone to her ear, and listened. Travis had come home to shower before work and found her note. His voicemails and texts ranged from disbelief and denial to anger and outrage. She rolled her eyes at his text reminding her that they were hosting thirty of his family members for Thanksgiving, as they did every year. *Would she be home?*

Unbelievable. Thanksgiving had been her favorite holiday—she loved cooking and the focus on family—until she'd married Travis. Her in-laws treated her like unpaid kitchen help and never lifted a finger to assist. She wasn't upset about missing the holiday "festivities"—she was elated.

Her fingers flew across the keyboard. She read her message, backspaced, and made a few adjustments.

No. You'll figure it out. I am done. We will not be spending any more holidays together. My lawyer will be in touch.

She pressed send. Clara replaced her phone in her purse and was zipping it shut when she heard it ping.

She pulled out her phone to see his response. It had not taken him long to get nasty.

Frozen all joint accounts. You'll have to contact me when you need money.

She typed back quickly.

No worries. I won't need anything from you. The house, its contents, and the accounts are all yours.

Clara opened the contacts on her phone, selected his number, and blocked it. She slid her phone into her purse and set off with a spring in her step that hadn't been there in a very long time.

Clara spent the best part of the next hour rummaging through the bags of clothes stuffed into her car. She wanted to come away with enough garments for the next ten days. The motel didn't have laundry facilities and she didn't fancy the idea of hiking to a laundromat—if there even was one close enough to the motel to make that feasible. She could wash her undies in the bathroom sink, if necessary.

She located her two recyclable shopping bags of toiletries and rearranged them so that one would stay with the car and one would come with her. She crammed what she wasn't taking to the motel back into the car and turned to the pile of items behind her. She had a large green trash bag full of clothes, two bed pillows, and the bag full of toiletries.

Clara positioned her purse strap around her neck, wearing it like a cross-body bag, and began gathering the items she'd chosen. Laden down like a pack mule, she moved slowly toward the road. She wasn't more than twenty feet from her car when the recyclable bag ripped, and her toiletries tumbled to the pavement. Her jar of expensive moisturizer cracked.

She stomped her foot in frustration and dropped the bag of clothes and her purse on the ground. She watched in horror as the pricey face cream oozed onto the asphalt.

She heard someone calling her name and looked up to see Andy approaching her. "Here, let me give you a hand with all that."

"No. Thank you. I've got this."

Andy bent from the waist and gathered her toiletries into one pile. He glanced up at her over the top of his glasses. "It's not a felony to accept help when it's offered, you know."

"No. Of course not. I'm sorry if I sound … ungrateful."

"I was just headed into town. I'll go get my car. We can pile all of this in the trunk, and I'll give you a lift to your motel." He straightened and faced her. "Would that be okay with you?"

Clara flushed. "Thank you. I'd appreciate that very much."

"You could have asked me for a ride—I'd have been happy to give you one."

"I … I didn't want to trouble you."

"It's no trouble. I'm driving right by."

He brought his car to where she stood, guarding her belongings, and in ten minutes she was inside her motel room.

Clara spent the remainder of the afternoon stowing her clothes in the small closet and dresser. When she was done, she propped herself up on the bed with pillows and grabbed the television remote. It had been years since she'd watched daytime television, and she was curious to see what was available to watch. She'd be spending a lot of time in this motel room. Twenty minutes later, she turned off the television and tossed the remote on the bed in disgust. As it turned out, daytime television was still the same terrible mix of talk shows, reruns, and infomercials that she remembered from her adolescence.

She opened her laptop and typed Pinewood into the search engine. There were a lot of places named Pinewood. She scrolled to the correct link and opened the town's official website. She soon learned that the town had been founded by ranchers and trappers more than a hundred and fifty years ago. The year-round population was seventy-five thousand. The public schools were ranked best in the region and a state university's main campus was located on the east side of town. She noted that she had missed their world-famous Harvest Festival, by a week. The photographs of the hilly terrain, blanketed with a mix of deciduous and pine trees, were spectacular.

Clara wondered idly if a college town, the size of Pinewood, could support a patisserie. When she'd investigated the business aspects of running a successful patisserie, the experts all recommended a potential customer base of at least two hundred thousand or more. She pursed her lips and closed her laptop. As pretty as Pinewood was, it would only be a stop on her way to her new home.

She glanced at the clock: four thirty. Heavy clouds were piling up in the west, blocking the setting sun and creating an early dusk. It might be a bit early for dinner, she reasoned, but if she went to the diner now, she would be sure to snag a table, and she'd enjoy watching how Johanson's Diner operated on a busy Friday night.

Clara entered the diner, picked up a menu from the stack next to the sign on the hostess stand that read "Seat Yourself" and found a table on the far-left side. From this vantage point, she could observe the front door, the lunch counter, and the swinging doors to the kitchen. The patisserie she planned to open might not be a restaurant, but she could always learn something new in any situation. Clara loved the food industry.

She'd been involved in food service since her teens, when she'd worked as a carhop on roller skates at the drive-in. She'd waited tables at a posh restaurant in college, and had managed the hospital cafeteria when she'd been employed as a dietician.

She opened her menu and marveled, once more, at the variety of ethnic dishes on the menu. The cooks here had to know more than how to operate a deep fryer or a grill. The inventory control alone on all of the ingredients would be mind-boggling

The door opened and a family of six stepped inside and headed for a corner booth. The father waved at a sturdy-looking waitress with a mix of black and magenta hair.

"The usual?" she called to him.

He nodded.

Two elderly couples and another young family followed closely on their heels.

The young waitress was ramping up her speed.

Clara closed her menu and set it on the table, signaling that she was ready to order.

The waitress, wearing a name tag that read "I'm Mary. What'll You Have?" set a glass of water in front of her.

"Hello. Have you been here long? I didn't see you come in."

"No worries. I'm not in a hurry. In fact, I was enjoying reading the menu."

The waitress's eyes widened in surprise. "I've not heard that before. I guess we do have a lot on there."

"What do you recommend?"

Mary shifted her weight from one foot to the other and tapped the eraser end of her pencil on her teeth. "Well … it's Friday, so we've got our fish fry goin' on." She gestured to the restaurant behind her. "That's what everybody comes for on Fridays. The fish is fresh and caught local. If you like fish, you won't find any better."

"Then I'll have that."

Mary scribbled on her order pad. "It's all you can eat, too."

"By the way, do you have any of that special cake left?"

Mary shook her head. "Sorry. It's all spoken for. People call in and reserve it ahead of time."

Clara had already polished off her slice of cake from lunch, and now she wished she'd thought to call ahead for another one.

Mary reached for her menu.

"Do you mind if I keep looking at this?" Clara asked.

"Sure, that's fine," Mary said in a voice that indicated she didn't understand Clara's interest in reading a menu.

Clara had her head bent over the menu, making mental lists of the various ingredients each one called for, when Josef stepped to her table.

"Good evening, Clara. I'm delighted to see you again. And so soon!"

Clara smiled up at him. "I'm glad to be back."

"Mary told me you're reading the menu? I don't think we've ever had anyone do that before."

"It's just that I'm a dietician—and I have a special interest in baking. I'm amazed by what you offer here."

"I'll pass that along to Maisie, too. She was so happy to hear your compliments about her cake." Josef beamed. "And now I can tell her that you're an expert."

"I don't know about that, but I do know my way around food."

The door opened and Kurt Holbrook stepped inside. He began looking for a place to sit.

Josef raised his hand and motioned for Kurt to join them. "We're all full," Josef said to Clara. "You wouldn't mind sharing your table with one of our regulars, would you?"

Clara opened her mouth to protest.

"It's our custom here on busy weekend nights," Josef went on. "What do they call it in sophisticated, foodie restaurants? A community table?"

Kurt shook Josef's hand and glanced down at Clara. "I can wait for a seat at the counter. I don't want to disturb you."

"Nonsense," Clara said. "I don't need to keep this whole table to myself. I was just reading the menu, anyway."

Kurt sat down across from her. "Great. I'll catch up on the news on my phone. We don't need to disturb each other."

Clara flipped to the third fold of the menu and continued her perusal while Kurt turned his attention to his phone.

Josef rolled his eyes. "I'd better get back to the kitchen. I'll be manning the fryer all night." He walked away, shaking his head.

Kurt had a standing order in for the Friday fish fry, and their meals arrived together. They ate without discussion, both engrossed in their reading. He broke the silence only to order a second cup of coffee, and Clara said good-bye after paying for her meal, wishing she had stopped eating after that second piece of fish. The batter had been so light and crispy and the fish so delicate and flaky that she couldn't resist a third piece. She was truly stuffed. If she had to eat every meal at Johanson's Diner for the duration of her stay in Pinewood, it would be no hardship.

She stood outside the entrance to the diner, winding her scarf around her neck, when she noticed a small sign in the window. She hadn't seen it when she'd come in.

The hand-printed white sign with large black letters said: "Help wanted—experienced cook urgently needed before Thanksgiving. Inquire within."

Clara paused. What else did she have to do to keep herself busy while she waited for her car to be repaired?

She liked this place—its vibe was warm and friendly. The food was worthy. She might even learn baking secrets from Maisie. Josef could certainly use the help.

Clara noted the posted restaurant hours. They started serving at seven. She'd be back at six the next morning to offer herself up as a cook. It would only be temporary, but she could help them through the Thanksgiving rush.

Chapter 5

Clara's breath froze in tiny droplets as she hurried across the parking lot to Johanson's Diner. Lights were on, confirming her suspicion that preparations were in full swing. She tried the front door but found it locked.

Clara walked around the outside of the building to a door marked: "Kitchen. Employees Only." A row of high windows along the back of the building shone with fluorescent lighting. The windows at one end were clouded with steam. Probably where the dishwasher was located, she surmised. Her pulse quickened. She loved the fast pace of a commercial kitchen, the choreographed symmetry of an experienced team of cooks.

She raised her hand to knock but thought better of it. Clara opened the door and stepped tentatively over the threshold.

Two middle-aged women in white coats and hair nets glanced at her. One was frying slabs of bacon on the grill while the other was tending to batter in a commercial-sized mixer. Neither moved from their post. The woman at the grill turned her head over her shoulder and called for Josef.

Josef quickly emerged from a walk-in cooler carrying six cardboard trays holding two dozen eggs each. His eyes widened at the sight of Clara before his characteristic smile graced his face.

"Good morning, Clara," he said as he set the stacked egg trays on a counter and came to her. "What can I do for you?"

"My goodness, you do work open to close, don't you?"

He shrugged. "That's the nature of this business."

She nodded. "I'm here to answer your advertisement for an experienced cook. As I said last night, I'm a dietician. I've worked food service my whole life. I'm a hard worker and a fast learner. I think I can help."

He rubbed his newly shaved chin as he ran his eyes over her face. "I thought you were only in Pinewood temporarily."

"I'll be here until my car gets repaired. That'll be the week after Thanksgiving."

"You're not on your way to family for the holiday?"

She shook her head emphatically no.

"I'm desperate for help next week," Josef murmured.

"Even if my car were, by some miracle, ready early, I wouldn't leave you in the lurch. I don't have anywhere I need to be. My time is my own these days. I'll bet you do a booming business on Thanksgiving."

"It's our busiest day of the year. We're only open from one until five and we do three seatings during that time. We offer a Thanksgiving meal with all the fixings. Payment is whatever the customer can afford. We take reservations but we always leave a few slots open at every sitting for drop-ins."

Clara unzipped her jacket and stuffed her gloves into the pockets. "That's a lovely thing to do. How many do you feed?"

"Last year, we had just over six hundred."

Clara took a step back. "Gosh. That's a lot."

Josef turned and motioned for her to follow him. "We don't have a food pantry in Pinewood, so we feed not only our regular customers, but also people who wouldn't get a meal without us."

Clara blinked hard. "That's the nicest thing I've heard in a long time."

"We expect to feed even more people this year." He pointed to a row of hooks along the wall. Three jackets hung neatly next to each other. "If you're serious, I'd be more than grateful for the help. Put your jacket and purse there."

Clara complied.

"We also distribute more than two hundred food boxes on the day before Thanksgiving for families that can't get out. We start with those at six a.m., so we're done before ten."

Clara stopped short. "You do food boxes, too? How in the world do you manage that? You must have extra help."

"We do. The boxes were Kurt Holbrook's idea. Remember him?"

Clara nodded.

"He takes care of all that. As a matter of fact, he finances most of the meals we serve to our less fortunate on Thanksgiving. He eats here and always leaves a more-than-generous tip. He's one of the best men I know."

"I'd love to help with all of this," Clara said.

"It's a tremendous amount of work," Josef said. "I'll expect long hours—one hundred ten percent effort."

"I'll give you all I've got," Clara said. "I'm used to working very hard at Thanksgiving, but this year, I think people may actually appreciate what I'm doing for them."

"I start cooks at double the minimum wage. I'm sure it's far less than you're accustomed to."

"That'll be just fine," Clara said. "And I'll donate my labor on Thanksgiving. You won't have to pay me for that day."

"I couldn't let you do that."

"I insist."

Josef grinned and held out his hand. "Welcome aboard, Clara Conway."

They shook hands.

"Where would you like me to start? I don't know your recipes or the flow of your kitchen, but I believe I already know how to operate all of your equipment."

Josef opened a thin metal cabinet, removed a clean white apron, and handed it to her. "There's a hairnet in the pocket. How are you at baking?"

"My specialty," she replied.

His grin widened. "Maisie is starting on the pies and other baked goods for the food boxes. She has helpers from our church, but no one who knows their way around a bakery. Would you mind working with her?"

Clara's heart soared. "I'd love to."

"I didn't want her involved this year, but she insisted. I worry that she'll overdo."

"I'll keep my eye on her," Clara said. "Maisie can give me direction, and I'll make sure that things are done to her satisfaction. She'll be in charge, but I won't let her lift a finger. At least, I'll try."

Josef swallowed hard. "You're the answer to my prayers, Clara," he said softly.

She blushed and turned her head aside.

"Our bakery is in the freestanding building along the back side of the property. She's there now, going over her lists and checking off ingredients. I'll take you over and introduce you, and I'll bring you both coffee and breakfast in about twenty minutes."

"Sounds great," Clara said, grabbing her jacket and purse back off of the hook, and following him out the door.

"What would you like to eat?" he asked.

"Surprise me," Clara said. "If I'm going to be one of the famous Johanson's Diner cooks, I'll need to be familiar with everything on the menu."

Maisie Johanson glanced up as the door to the bakery opened. A shot of cold air scattered the invoices she had been checking on the long butcher block worktable. She lunged and grabbed them before they floated to the floor.

A smile that reached her clear blue eyes brightened her face. She straightened, still clutching her papers, and swept a blond tendril now generously mixed with gray back into the bun at the nape of her neck.

"I've got a surprise for you," Josef said, "and I know you're going to like it."

Maisie stepped around the worktable to join them.

"I'd like you to meet Clara Conway," Josef said. "She's the woman I was telling you about—the one who liked your cake so much."

"I remember. I'm glad you enjoyed it." She turned to her husband, a question in her eyes.

"Clara's going to be joining us as our new cook," Josef said. "At least for the time being, while she's …" he paused, choosing his words, "temporarily staying in Pinewood."

"That's wonderful," Maisie said. "My Josef works way too hard. He needs help but it's impossible to find experienced cooks around here."

"I'm thrilled to be working with you," Clara said. "I'm extremely impressed with the variety and quality of the food I've had at the diner. If you were located in a large metropolitan area, your walls would be full of awards."

Maisie and Josef exchanged a proud smile.

"She'll be with us through Thanksgiving and knows how to operate all of our equipment. Best of all, her specialty is baking. I thought I'd start her out here, to give you a hand with all the pies and dinner rolls we turn out for the food boxes and the meal on Thursday."

Maisie arched her brows at her husband. "You're worried that this is too much for me, aren't you?"

Josef turned his head aside. "I didn't say that, but you're still regaining your strength."

"Let's play it by ear," Clara broke in. "I'll start here, with you, and if everything's running smoothly and you don't need my help, I'll head back to the diner." She unzipped her jacket and walked to a row of hooks along the wall.

Josef swept his wife into his arms. "I have a feeling about Clara," he whispered into Maisie's ear. "I think she'll be with us a lot longer than she's planning on."

Maisie kissed his cheek. "I hope you're right," she whispered back. "I like her already. And whether she's with you or me, we both need the help."

"I'll leave the two of you to get started," Josef said as he headed for the door.

Clara tucked her hair into the net. "What have you got planned for today?" She pointed to the large cans of pumpkin lined up against the wall. "I'm guessing pumpkin pies?"

Maisie nodded approvingly. The girl was observant and smart. "Two hundred of them—for the food boxes that we'll give out on Wednesday."

"And you say you've got helpers from your church coming in? We're not turning out two hundred pies, just the two of us?"

Maisie snorted. "Do you think we could do that, without help?"

"I know we could," Clara replied. "Pumpkin is easy to do in bulk. Now if we had to peel apples for that many pies, it'd be another story."

"I like your confidence," Maisie said.

"I've spent years supervising the kitchen of a five-hundred bed hospital. We served holiday meals to patients and staff—and all of our pies were made on site." She smiled at Maisie. "We've got this. How many helpers will be pitching in?"

"I'm expecting ten ladies—all excellent home cooks."

"Piece of cake! Pardon the pun."

"I've just double-checked our inventory. We've got everything we'll need between now and Thanksgiving."

"What's your total planned production?"

"Two hundred pumpkin pies today, four hundred tomorrow and Monday, three hundred apple pies on Monday, and six hundred dozen dinner rolls on Tuesday and Wednesday."

Maisie leaned over the worktable and rested her head in her hands.

Clara put her arm around the older woman's shoulders. "All that sounds doable to me."

Maisie swiveled her neck to look up at Clara. "You sound confident."

"I am. Will your church helpers be here every day?"

Maisie nodded.

"Why don't I go wash my hands while you get your recipes? It's time we got started. I'll put the ingredients into the mixers, so the crust is ready when our helpers arrive."

"We've got forty-pound bags of flour. I can't help you lift them. We'll need to wait for the others to arrive."

"Nonsense," Clara replied. "I can handle them on my own."

The lines on Maisie's forehead eased. "I could hoist a large bag of flour when I was your age, too. Not anymore." She sighed heavily. "The hand-washing sink's in the far corner." Her eyes flickered over Clara's left hand. "That's a lovely wedding ring. You'll have to take it off while you're working. I'll lock it up for you in the desk in my office in back."

Clara looked down at her hand, staring at the ring. She began twisting and tugging, until it finally slipped over her knuckle and off her finger.

Clara placed the symbol of a marriage that she no longer wanted into the palm of Maisie's outstretched hand.

"Keep it," Clara said quietly.

"What do you mean?"

"I'm … I'm divorcing my husband, and I'm not going to put that ring back on my finger."

Maisie took a step back. "Surely you'll want it back—whether you wear it or not." She brought the ring into the light that was streaming through the windows. "These are lovely diamonds. Couldn't you have them reset into a new piece of jewelry?"

Clara shook her head emphatically no. "I don't want them near me in any way, shape, or form."

"How long have you been … separated, if I might ask?"

"It's been … recent."

"Then why don't you hang onto this ring until you've had time to let things settle in your mind. You wouldn't want to make a rash decision."

A smile crept across Clara's face. "I've got the perfect use for them, already. Is there a jeweler in town that would buy them? I'd like to donate the money to help underwrite the community Thanksgiving meal that you provide."

Maisie stared at Clara.

"You do need extra money, to help with the food boxes and to cover the meals that people can't pay for on Thursday, don't you? You lose money on all of this, don't you?"

"Well … yes."

"Then there we are. I'll give you the ring, and you can sell it."

"My sister and brother-in-law are the most reputable jewelers in the county. They'll give you a fair price."

"Perfect." Clara pushed the ring back into Maisie's palm and curled Maisie's fingers around it. "It's yours now."

"What about if you change your mind? You and your husband reconcile?"

Clara's expression hardened. "I'm not going to change my mind. My marriage is over."

Chapter 6

"You're dressed mighty casual," Josef said, filling a mug with steaming coffee and setting it on the counter in front of Kurt. "I've never known you to wear jeans to the office on a weekday."

"I'm not working today," Kurt replied, cupping the warm mug with his cold hands. "I decided to take the day off to help you and Maisie with the food boxes for tomorrow. I heard you could use an extra pair of hands."

"That's awfully nice of you."

"How's Maisie doing? Did she get enough help in the bakery?"

"The church folk came through for her, but the biggest help has been Clara Conway."

Kurt narrowed his eyes. "Who's she?"

"Just the beautiful brunette I introduced you to last Friday night, at that table right over there." He pointed over Kurt's shoulder to the table that Kurt and Clara had shared.

Kurt nodded. "That's right. I got the impression she was just passing through."

"She hasn't 'passed through' yet. She's been a godsend to Maisie and me. She knows her way around a kitchen, let me tell you. She and Maisie are getting along like a house on fire. Maisie's spirits are the highest they've been since she had the stroke. Those two both love to bake, and they chatter nonstop about ideas they've read about or seen on that British baking show."

"I'm happy to hear it. Sounds like this Clara is what Maisie needed." He lifted the mug to his lips and took a tentative sip, making sure he didn't scald his mouth.

"She might be what you need, too," Josef said quietly.

Kurt put up a hand. "Don't go there, Josef. I'm fine as I am."

"You and Rachel were happy. Don't you want that with someone else? She told me she wanted you to remarry." Josef leaned toward Kurt. "She died three years ago. Isn't it time to move on?"

"Even if it were, I'm not going to 'move on' with a married woman." Kurt raised an eyebrow at Josef. "She was wearing a wedding ring, Josef. She's married."

"She's getting a divorce. She gave that ring to Maisie to sell, and she's donating the money for the food boxes and Thursday's meal." Josef crossed his arms over his chest. "You've got nothing to worry about."

"The last thing I need is someone on the rebound. No thank you," Kurt said. "Besides, she barely noticed me when we ate together the other night. She's clearly not interested in romance. Or at least not in romance with me."

"I don't know about that. Maisie and I talked about it last night. We both think the two of you would make the perfect couple."

Kurt slid off the stool and placed a five-dollar bill on the counter.

Josef picked it up and stuffed it into Kurt's shirt pocket. "You're taking time away from your law practice to be here. The least I can do is buy you a cup of coffee."

"Thanks. Now—what do you need help with?"

A tiny smile played at Josef's lips. "Maisie just texted. They need two more forty-pound bags of flour. They're around back, in the receiving area. Would you mind taking them to the bakery?"

"Sure."

"And if you run into Clara while you're over there, it wouldn't hurt you to smile at her."

Kurt shook his head and his mouth was stern, but his eyes were smiling.

He went to the receiving area, hoisted one bag onto his shoulder, and walked to the bakery.

Maisie saw him approaching and opened the door for him, directing him to place it at the end of the long worktable.

Kurt wove through the workers, all busily concentrating on their tasks, as he made his way to the spot Maisie designated. He searched through the controlled chaos in front of him but didn't see Clara.

Kurt was leaving the bakery after depositing the second bag of flour when Clara came around a corner, head down, concentrating on a canister of milk that she was carrying to the stove.

She became aware of his presence too late, colliding with him and slopping milk down the front of his heavy woolen shirt.

"Oh my gosh," she said, looking up in surprise. "I'm so sorry! Are you okay? I was trying to get this ..." she looked at the almost empty canister. "It doesn't matter. Look at you. I've made a mess of your shirt."

Kurt glanced down at his sodden shirt and tried to wipe the milk away. "It was an accident. No worries."

"It was completely my fault. Let me get you a towel."

"I'll take care of it. You probably needed that for something you're making," he pointed around the room. "I'll let you get back to it."

"We are busy. Thank you."

Kurt made his exit.

Clara retraced her steps, in search of more milk.

Maisie intercepted her. "I see you were having a nice conversation with that handsome Kurt Holbrook."

"I spilled milk all over his shirt, Maisie. That's hardly a conversation."

"Still, he's an awfully nice young man. We've been friends forever. I'm glad you're getting to know him."

"I don't think ruining his shirt constitutes getting to know him." Clara patted her new friend on the elbow. "I've got to replace this milk. They're waiting on me." With that, she dismissed any thought of the attractive young attorney and returned to the task at hand.

Chapter 7

Clara raised the mug of coffee, prepared using her in-room coffee maker, and sniffed the complimentary brew. It smelled stale and unappealing, but she took a swig of the murky liquid, anyway. It was ten minutes after five in the morning, and she needed caffeine.

She'd promised Josef she would meet him at the diner at five thirty. She'd be on hand to assist with distribution of the food boxes and, when they were done, she'd help Maisie in the bakery.

She picked up her phone to check the day's forecast on her weather app and was surprised to see that she had two unread text messages waiting for her. Since she'd blocked Travis's number, she'd had no messages from anyone.

The first was from her only real friend at the hospital. Marilyn asked how she was doing and when she'd be back to work, before wishing her a Happy Thanksgiving. It was clear that no one at work had mentioned to Marilyn that Clara had quit.

For the first time since she'd made the sudden decision to leave town, she felt a pang of regret. She missed Marilyn. Clara hesitated, her fingers hovering over her keyboard. She didn't have time right now to explain her actions to Marilyn—and didn't know what she would say about them, even if she did. Clara typed, "Happy Thanksgiving. We've got a lot to catch up on. Talk next week?" She added a happy face emoji, and pressed send.

The second message was from her attorney. He'd prepared drafts of her divorce papers while he was out of town, and his paralegal would be forwarding them to her via email before noon. He asked her to review them carefully and make a note of any questions she might have. They would go over them when he was back in the office after Thanksgiving.

Clara bit her lip. Since her marriage to Travis, the night before Thanksgiving usually found her hard at work, in her kitchen, preparing a holiday dinner for her ungrateful, ill-mannered in-laws. She was relieved to be out from under that burden but wasn't sure that reviewing divorce papers was much of an improvement. Still, it had to be done and she had nothing else on her agenda that evening. She might as well get it over with.

Clara chucked her phone into her purse, slipped into her down jacket, and pulled her knit cap down around her ears. The weather app had reported a temperature of twenty-nine degrees, and she assumed she'd be working outside this morning. She wound her scarf around her neck and headed across the parking lot to the diner.

She skirted the front, where the sign in the window glowed with the word "Closed" and stepped into the sea of activity at the back.

Four white tents, with the sides rolled up, had been erected next to the driveway leading off the main road to the diner. Portable lights illuminated men arranging cardboard boxes into tall stacks inside the tents. A long, rectangular table ran the length of the first tent. Signs that read "A-H," "I-Q," and "R-Z" were placed evenly along the table. A clipboard with lined sheets of paper and pens sat in front of the signs.

Large, directional arrows had been painted on the driveway that ran past the tents.

The backdoor to the diner was propped open, despite the cold, and light spilled onto a tall coffee urn set up just outside the door. Steam rose from the top of the urn. The breath of the man standing next to it turned immediately into frost.

Clara recognized Josef and walked toward him.

His face broke into a broad grin as soon as she stepped out of the shadow. "Clara! Good morning." He stamped his feet. "It's colder than we expected. I didn't know if we'd see you this early."

"I told you I'd be here," Clara said. "I helped bake every pie in those boxes," she continued. "I'm excited to be here to give them away."

"That's the spirit," Josef said. "Would you like a cup of coffee?"

"I had one from the machine in my motel room."

Josef pulled a face. "That stuff doesn't count as coffee." He dispensed fragrant brown liquid into a mug. "Here. You'll need this. We begin handing out boxes at six thirty. They'll be lining up any minute now."

She took the mug, glad for the warmth that seeped through her gloves, and took a sip.

"What would you like me to do?"

"Kurt's in charge of distribution," Josef said. "He's around here somewhere. I told him you were coming to help. He said he'll have you check off the names of people as they arrive."

"That's all of them," a man called.

Kurt walked toward them, motioning for the men who had been stacking boxes to gather round.

Clara smiled at him. His face was in shadow and she couldn't see if he returned her smile.

"Okay, everybody," he said. "We'll handle this just like last year. A car will drive up, and we'll get the family's last name. There'll be three people working the sign-in table." He pointed to Clara and two of the men. "You'll find the family's name, and the list will tell you whether they get one or two boxes. It's all based on family size." He paused and looked at Clara and the other two. "Make sense?"

They nodded.

"The box handlers will be behind you. You'll tell the next handler in line how many boxes go in the car. You'll ask the driver to pop the trunk. The handler will load the box or boxes and shut the trunk. The family will drive away."

Headlights from the first car of the day swung off the road and onto the driveway.

"Looks like it's almost showtime," Kurt said. He checked his watch. "It's six fifteen."

A steady stream of cars began inching slowly up the driveway.

"Let's try to get this done as fast as possible. Accept people's thanks, but keep the line moving." He swung his eyes across the volunteers lined up in front of him. "Any questions?"

Clara hesitated, then held up her hand. "What if the family isn't on our list? Do we turn them … away?"

"No. We don't want anyone in that line to leave here without a box of food. We have extras. If you think you're going to run out, let me know. I've got grocery store gift cards, just in case."

He gestured to the first car in line to move forward.

The car pulled up to the table and the driver rolled down his window. He gave his name to the man next to Clara.

Clara overheard Josef, as he clapped Kurt on the back. "Grocery gift cards? That's a new one this year. Purchased by you, I'll guess."

"We were a few boxes short last year," she heard Kurt say.

"Which you remedied with cash out of your own pocket, as I remember. You're a good man, Kurt. Your folks would be very proud of you."

The two men moved out of earshot and Clara walked up to the next car in line.

Chapter 8

Maisie stepped to the middle of the bakery workroom and clapped her hands over her head. "Okay, everybody, that's a wrap."

A cheer went up from the bakery staff, comprised of three full-time workers, plus Maisie and Clara. The church volunteers had departed when the pies for the food boxes had been completed. It had been up to the five of them to produce all of the pies and dinner rolls to be served the next day.

"It's just after four thirty," Maisie continued. "We finished in record time this year."

"Thanks to Clara," one of the women said. "You're a pie crust wizard."

Clara laughed and waved away the compliment. "It's something I enjoy."

"She's right," Maisie said. "You've got a real feel for baking. And you're calm under pressure."

Clara flushed. "Coming from you, Maisie, that means a lot."

Maisie turned to the other bakers, now gathered in front of her. "As you know, the diner closes early on the day before Thanksgiving. Josef's picked up pizza for everyone. He always buys way more than we need. Feel free to head on over to the diner to eat with us or grab a pizza to take home to your family."

"Thank you, Maisie," murmured the other bakers.

"It's the least we can do, after all of your hard work these last few days. You shouldn't have to cook tonight."

Maisie took Clara's elbow. "Come on over and sit with Josef and me."

"I'd like that," Clara said. She extended her arm to steady Maisie. "You've been on your feet almost all day. You must be exhausted."

"I think adrenaline got me through," Maisie said, "but I'm feeling it now."

"Where's your cane?"

"I forgot it when I left the house."

"Take my arm, and we'll make our way to the diner."

The two women walked slowly across the rear parking lot to the diner. They entered through the kitchen, where the cooks were helping themselves to slices of pizza from the boxes that lined the counter.

Kurt was in the far corner of the kitchen, handing out boxes of pizza to the workers who were taking them home.

Josef rushed over to his wife. "Are you all right? You overdid it, didn't you?"

She looked up at him and leaned in to kiss his cheek. "I'm tired, I'll admit. But I did what I love doing and that felt great."

Josef steered her into a seat at the first table outside the kitchen. "You stay right here, and I'll bring you a plate. What do you want?"

"It all smells delicious. Surprise me."

Josef returned to the kitchen and picked two paper plates from the stack at the end of the counter. He handed one to Clara. "Help yourself. I'm going to get some for Maisie. You can sit with her, and I'll join you in a minute."

"Thank you," Clara said, taking the plate. "It looks—and smells—amazing."

"Our local pizzeria could hold its own against any of the fancy big-city ones." He pointed to an ice chest on the floor. "Sodas are over there."

Clara and Josef moved along the counter. Clara selected a slice of traditional sausage and pepperoni and a veggie piled high with peppers, broccoli, and Brussels sprouts.

She pulled a diet cola out of the cooler and followed Josef to the table.

Maisie was slumped back in her chair, her eyes closed.

"Sweetheart," Josef said quietly as he placed her plate in front of her.

Maisie's eyes flew open and she blinked. "I nodded off, didn't I? I guess I'm more tuckered out than I thought."

"I never should have let you come in for all of this," Josef said. "I should have hired someone to run the bakery."

"Oh, hush," Maisie said. "Clara was a huge help. I couldn't have done it without her, that's for sure." She smiled at Clara, who had slipped into the chair next to her. "I just need a good night's sleep, and I'll be right as rain."

Josef hovered over her.

"Go get yourself something to eat."

He nodded and went back into the kitchen, reappearing moments later with Kurt. Both men balanced plates loaded with pizza.

"Hello, dear," Maisie said to Kurt. "You're still here? The food boxes were done by noon."

"I took the day off, and there was still a lot to do to get ready for tomorrow."

"He's been a terrific help, as usual," Josef said. He looked between Clara and Kurt. "You both have. Maisie and I are very grateful."

"I'll always be here for you," Kurt said. He lifted his eyes to Clara. "I'm not happy that you had car trouble, but I'm sure glad that you've been here to work with Maisie this week."

"It's been my pleasure." She fidgeted with her paper napkin. "Being here—feeling needed and being part of this effort—has been a blessing to me."

Maisie raised a quizzical eyebrow at Josef, and he nodded imperceptibly in response.

Josef checked his watch and stood suddenly. "I need to nip over to the animal shelter to drop off a stray dog that's been hanging around the dumpsters all week. I finally caught him. It's too cold for the creature to spend another night outside."

"Will they still be open this late?"

"I called and Josie said that she'll be there until six, feeding the animals. If I leave now, I'll be there in time to drop him off." He turned to his tablemates. "You enjoy the rest of your supper, and I'll be right back."

"I've got a better idea," Kurt said, gathering up the empty paper plates from the table. "Why don't you and Maisie drop the dog off at the shelter and then head on home?"

"I've got to come back to clear away all of the pizza trash and lock up," Josef said.

"I remember how to do that," Kurt said. "It hasn't been that many years since I worked my way through law school on the diner's evening shift."

"But you've been here since before dawn," Josef protested.

"And so have both of you." Kurt helped Maisie to her feet. "Go on. I've got this covered."

"I don't have anything planned for this evening," Clara said, glad for an excuse to put off the task of reviewing her divorce papers. "I'll help Kurt get the kitchen back in order. Between the two of us, it won't take more than twenty minutes."

"If you're sure?" Josef asked.

"We're sure," Kurt and Clara replied in unison.

Josef and Maisie headed for his car where the stray, secure in a carrier that had a permanent spot in Josef's backseat, waited for them.

"I'll get a couple of trash bags," Kurt said.

Clara followed him into the kitchen. "There's enough slices left over to form an entire pizza. I'll put them into one box, and you can take them home … to your family."

Kurt shook his head. "It's just me, and I won't eat them. Take them to the motel. I'll bet someone there will want them."

"Good idea," Clara said, "I hate wasting food." She began placing stray slices of pizza into one box, while Kurt put the empty boxes, cups, and napkins into a trash bag.

"I'm sorry that you're stuck here and won't get home for Thanksgiving," he said, cutting his eyes to her.

"I don't have a home to go to right now." She turned her back to him as she swept empty soda cans to the edge of the counter. "Being here for the holiday is as good a place as any."

"Weren't you on your way somewhere?"

"I was driving west and wasn't going to stop until I discovered a place that called to me; that resonated with me and made me want to stay."

"Sounds pretty adventurous."

Clara looked over her shoulder at him and laughed. "No one's ever called me adventurous before." She rested one hand on the counter and stood straighter. "But I guess it is. I'm getting a divorce and decided to start over, someplace new."

"Was Pinewood calling to you?"

"No. I was forced to stop because my alternator gave out."

Kurt nodded and deposited the soda cans in his trash bag.

"The people *are* very friendly—I've seen that already." She picked up a bottle of disinfectant spray and spritzed the now-empty counter. "But I'm a big-city girl, so I'll be on my way as soon as my car gets fixed. Are you from this area?"

Kurt began wiping the counter. "I went to law school here. I met Josef and Maisie's daughter working at the diner. We got married and I started my law practice in Pinewood."

Clara stopped spritzing the counter and faced him. "I thought you said you were alone?"

"Rachel died three years ago. Cancer."

"Oh, Kurt … I'm so sorry to hear that."

He nodded and kept wiping the counter.

"The last two years of her life were rough. Josef and Maisie were devoted to her. We were all devastated when she died. The experience bound us together. I'm closer to them than I am to my own family."

"It's obvious they think the world of you."

"The feeling is mutual." He tossed his rag into a metal bin by the sink and hefted the two bags of trash he'd collected. "It looks pretty good, don't you think?'

Clara scanned the room. "Yep. Our work here is done."

He gestured to the door with his head. "Let's go. We've got a very busy day tomorrow."

"I'm looking forward to it," Clara said and meant it. For the first time in years, she was excited about cooking Thanksgiving dinner. She picked up the box of leftover pizza that she had set aside. "What time do we start?"

"Josef and I will be here at five thirty. The first seating is at one."

"Then I'll see you at five thirty."

Their footsteps reverberated in the still night as they walked across the asphalt. Kurt veered off, toward the dumpster.

Clara continued across the parking lot to the motel. When she reached the entrance, she turned back toward the diner.

Kurt stood by the only car in the lot, watching her walk.

She raised her hand over her head and waved at him.

He waved back and got into his car.

He'd watched her walk home, Clara thought. Like Andy, he'd made sure she was safe. Despite the cold night, she suddenly felt warm.

She entered the lobby of the motel and walked up to the night desk clerk, holding out the pizza box. "Are you hungry? I've got an extra."

The young man pushed his college textbook aside and stood, a smile spreading wide across his face. "I got out of class late and didn't have time to stop for dinner. I'm starved."

"Enjoy," she said as the beaming young man took the box.

"Thank you," he said. "And Happy Thanksgiving."

Chapter 9

Clara blew a tendril of hair off of her forehead as she stirred a vat of gravy simmering on the stove. She picked up a clean spoon, dipped it into the steaming golden brown liquid, and brought it to her lips. "Yes," she said, nodding and smiling at the cook hovering over the pot. "That's done it."

The cook raised an eyebrow. "Really? It's not too salty?"

"Taste it for yourself," she said, pointing to a jar containing the tasting spoons.

He did as she suggested. "I can't believe you saved this. I thought I'd ruined it, and we'd run out of gravy. On Thanksgiving!"

"Cutting up a potato and stirring it into the gravy absorbed the excess salt. I learned that trick from my mother. All you have to do now is fish the potato pieces out of the gravy and throw them away. Problem solved."

"Will do. Thank you, Clara."

Maisie stepped into the kitchen and motioned for Clara to join her.

Clara patted him lightly on the shoulder as she moved around the cook and made her way to Maisie.

"I've been looking for you. I hear you've been working like a fiend," Maisie said. "Josef and I are very grateful."

"I'm having the best Thanksgiving I've had in years," Clara said.

"I can't imagine that," Maisie said.

"It's a long story, and not worth repeating," Clara replied. "What do you need?"

"We always eat our Thanksgiving dinner at the middle seating," Maisie said. "It's our least busy time, and we're not going to do all this cooking without sitting down to a proper meal ourselves."

"Rightly so," Clara said.

"Josef and I would like you to join us."

"I don't want to intrude," Clara said.

"Nonsense," Maisie said, pointing to Clara's apron and hairnet. "Take those off and come join us. The table's all set, and we're waiting for you."

"But …"

"I'm not taking no for an answer."

Clara began untying her apron and laughed. "Okay, okay. To be honest, I'm starved. Everything smells so good."

The two women exited the kitchen and crossed to a booth in the corner. Josef stood to allow Maisie to slide in next to him.

Clara was taking her seat across from Josef and Maisie when Kurt walked up. She looked at him, startled. "Oh … Happy Thanksgiving."

"The same to you," he said, turning wide eyes to Josef and Maisie.

"We're the only people Clara knows in town," Maisie said. "We didn't want her to have to eat with strangers."

"No. Of course not," Kurt said.

"Why don't you scoot over, dear, so that Kurt can sit next to you? They're bringing our salads to the table, now."

Clara moved down the bench and Kurt sat.

Josef's smile was like a benediction. "We're glad the two of you could join us."

The foursome enjoyed a traditional Thanksgiving meal that was as good as any presented by an establishment boasting a Michelin star. Josef sang the praises of Pinewood in a manner that would have done the chamber of commerce proud.

"This turkey is so moist and flavorful," Clara commented between mouthfuls.

"We use fresh, locally raised birds that we brine ourselves," Josef said.

"It's great—as always," Kurt said. "For me, the gravy is the standout this year."

Maisie winked at Clara. "That's because of Clara, I think. She was doing something to it when I came into the kitchen to fetch her for dinner. Was there a problem you were fixing?"

"Nothing that doesn't happen to every cook, now and again," Clara said.

"I agree, the gravy is fabulous," Josef said. "If we've got any left over, I'm taking it home and having slices of bread swimming in this gravy as a bedtime snack."

"That's about the worst thing you could eat," Maisie fussed at him.

"I only do it once a year," Josef protested.

Maisie rubbed his arm. "All right. I know you've been eating gravy bread since you were a little boy."

Dessert arrived with pieces of both pumpkin and apple pie on each plate, whipped cream topping the pumpkin, and vanilla ice cream next to the apple.

Clara groaned. "I don't think I can eat another bite."

"They smell incredible," Kurt said, inhaling. "Maisie makes the best pies in the state."

"Clara made these," Maisie replied.

They picked up their forks and dove into the irresistible sweets.

"Maisie has been singing your praises," Josef said. "You're welcome to work at the diner as long as you're in Pinewood, and we hope that's a long time."

Clara was lifting a forkful of apple pie to her mouth when Andy Rodriquez approached their booth. "Sorry to disturb you," Andy said. "I saw Clara was with you." He directed his words to her. "I forgot to call you yesterday, but your parts came in late in the afternoon. We're closed this weekend, but I'll work on your car first thing Monday morning. I should have it repaired and ready to go by noon."

Clara put her fork down on her plate. "Thank you," she said quietly.

"I'm glad you got to have a nice Thanksgiving dinner while you were in Pinewood," Andy said, smiling at the others in the booth. "I'll have you out of here and back on the road before you know it. I'll call as soon as I'm done."

"That's … wonderful," Clara said.

Andy turned and walked away.

Clara lowered her eyes to the table, then pushed her plate away. "I really can't manage another mouthful."

Kurt looked at his watch. "I think we'd better clear out so the servers can reset the table for the last seating." He turned to Clara. "I'm going fishing with one of my partners this weekend and won't be back until late Monday. You'll be on your way by then, so… good luck with your journey. I hope that the rest of it goes smoothly, and that you end up exactly where you're meant to be."

Maisie and Josef exchanged quizzical glances.

"Thank you," Clara said. "Have a nice weekend. I hope they're biting."

Chapter 10

Clara hovered her mouse over the Submit button, then clicked to return the signed verification of her divorce petition to her attorney. She'd gotten up early to review the papers. Her attorney had prepared everything to her satisfaction. It was Monday morning and the courthouse would be open. It was time to file the papers and make an official end to a marriage commitment that Travis had dishonored for years.

She shut her laptop and went to the window of her motel room, drawing aside the heavy draperies. The rising sun shone brightly, turning the frost-covered grass into an iridescent carpet. The weather forecast had been accurate— freezing rain had fallen on Pinewood over the weekend, leaving a spectacularly clear autumn morning in its wake. It would be a lovely day to continue her journey westward.

She turned and surveyed the room behind her. She'd worked long hours at the diner over the weekend and hadn't gotten around to packing up her things until Sunday evening. She'd been surprised at how many of her belongings she'd scattered around the motel room in her short stay there. Her suitcases, purse, laptop, and a shopping bag with her toiletries were lined up, ready for departure, on the right side of the door.

She checked her watch. It was almost ten thirty. With any luck, she'd have her car by noon. The breakfast rush at the diner should be over. She'd stop in to pick up her wages, which Josef had insisted he'd have ready for her, eat a late breakfast, and say her goodbyes to Josef and Maisie.

She blinked hard as she thought of the elderly couple who had shown her such kindness. She'd known them less than two weeks, yet they'd taken up residence in her heart.

Clara shook herself out of her reverie and snatched her jacket from the chair where she'd deposited it the night before. Her future was sure to be in a large urban area, where there would be enough customers to support the patisserie she planned to start with the seed money she'd inherited from her mother. There was no point moping around her motel room, feeling maudlin about the people she'd miss in Pinewood. It had been a wonderful community to be stuck in while her car was being repaired, but like the first person one dates after a breakup, it wasn't the one to commit to for the rest of her life.

She stepped out into the deceptively cold air, the bright sun doing nothing to warm the day. She made her way swiftly across the almost deserted parking lot and climbed the steps to the front door of the diner.

Maisie and Josef were seated next to each other at the counter, enjoying cups of coffee.

Clara stepped around the vacant hostess station and made her way to them.

Maisie started to get off of the counter stool, but Clara gestured to her to stay put. Clara leaned in and hugged the older woman.

"You're here for your check," Josef said. "We were beginning to think you weren't going to stop by before you left town."

Clara cocked her head to one side. "You know I wouldn't leave without saying goodbye."

"We hoped not," Maisie said, taking Clara's hand in her own and squeezing it.

Josef pulled an envelope from his pocket and handed it to her. "Here's your wages, plus a tiny little bit extra."

"What? You didn't need to do that!"

"It's not much," Josef said. "Just enough to buy you dinner wherever you're going. We want you to know how much we appreciated your help."

"You were a lifesaver, dear," Maisie said, brushing a hand over her eyes. "I loved working with you. It was like …" Her voice broke. "Well … let's just say that standing next to you brought back memories."

"Thank you," Clara replied. She bit her lower lip, remembering the countless times she'd stood next to her mother in their kitchen when she was growing up. "I meant it when I said I had the best Thanksgiving of my adult life. I'm the one who's grateful to you for taking me under your wing."

"Is your car ready?" Josef asked.

"I'm expecting to hear any minute now. I thought I'd come over to get a late breakfast before I leave town," she continued in a rush, "and say goodbye."

Josef reached behind him and grabbed a menu from behind the counter. He pressed it into her hands. "Order whatever you'd like. It's on the house."

"And we'll send you with today's special dessert—it's a pumpkin cake with maple icing—to take with you."

Clara's phone began ringing in her purse. "That's probably Andy, telling me my car's ready." She foraged in her purse, bringing the phone out on the fourth ring. She swiped at the screen and brought the phone to her cheek.

"Hi, Andy," she said. "Am I all set?"

Josef and Maisie watched her expression change as Clara listened to Andy on the other end of the line.

"All right," Clara said. "I'll wait to hear from you."

She turned to Josef and Maisie, a slight smile playing at her lips.

"That was Andy at the garage?" Maisie asked.

Clara nodded. "My car isn't ready. They sent the wrong part."

Maisie gripped her coffee cup to prevent herself from clapping her hands.

"So you'll have to stay a while longer?"

"I'm afraid so."

"Did he tell you how long it will take to get the right one?"

"He said that he'll try to get it sent by overnight courier, but that it could be another week."

"For an alternator?" Josef asked.

"I have a foreign car. Parts are always an issue."

"I'm sorry to hear that." Josef stopped abruptly and a grin spread from ear to ear. "That's a lie. No, I'm not. Does this mean you'll come back to work with us until it's ready?"

Maisie turned bright eyes on Clara.

Clara wanted to throw her arms around the pair and hug them. "If you'll have me."

"Order yourself some breakfast," Josef said. "I'm not reneging on my offer."

"When you're done, come to my office in the bakery," Maisie said. "I'd like to go over this week's dessert specials."

"I can't think of anything I'd rather do," Clara said. "I'll bring my food over, and we can get started while I eat."

Josef looked at the happy countenance of the woman he'd loved for decades. Clara might be leaving in another week, but she was here now, and his Maisie was happier than she'd been since Rachel's death.

Chapter 11

Clara glanced at the clock on the wall of the bakery building. She'd made excellent progress on the puff pastry she'd prepared to show Maisie when the older woman got back from her dental appointment.

Maisie had dismissed Clara's suggestion that they make their own puff pastry for the chocolate hazelnut mousse cups that were on the menu as Friday's featured dessert, declaring it was too much work.

Maybe it was the influence of binge-watching episodes of *The Great British Baking Show* on her laptop every night in her motel room, but Clara was determined to demonstrate how easy—and inexpensive—it was to make it from scratch.

She took a ball of pastry and began rolling it out. Clara was alone in the bakery. The tick of the large clock on the wall was the only sound other than the soft rumble of the refrigerator's compressor.

Clara found the tactile pleasure of working with the dough calming. She began singing, softly under her breath, a hymn that her mother always sang when working in the kitchen. She reached for a large slab of butter, placed it on top of the rolled-out pastry, covered it with plastic wrap, and began whacking the butter with her rolling pin to distribute it evenly across the dough. She folded the pastry over the butter, sealed the edges, and rolled it out before folding it into thirds again. She was so engrossed in her task that she didn't hear Maisie slip in the back door of the bakery.

"I've got peace like a river," Maisie joined in.

Clara looked up suddenly and stopped singing. "I didn't hear you come in."

"You were busy," Maisie said, pointing to the dough. "Is that what I think it is?"

Clara nodded as she encased the pastry in plastic wrap. "I hope you don't mind, but I love to make my own pastry, and I had the time."

"That won't be enough for all of the mousse cups we'll need to make tomorrow," Maisie said.

Clara took her wrapped pastry to the refrigerator and motioned for Maisie to follow her. She opened the fridge, pointing to the other similar packages inside. "I made all of these."

Maisie took a step back. "You are amazing."

"Everyone gets freaked out about puff pastry, but it's easy once you get the hang of it." She smiled over her shoulder at Maisie. "Are you up for trying this out tomorrow?"

"I most certainly am," Maisie said, leaning her elbow onto the counter. "Coming in here and listening to you sing that hymn took me back to my mother's kitchen. She's the one who taught me to bake. If she was in the kitchen, she was singing hymns."

"That's funny," Clara said. "Mine did that, too. "'Peace Like a River' was her favorite. I didn't realize I was singing it."

"That's one more thing we have in common," Maisie said.

"Is there anything else I can do for you this afternoon?" Clara asked.

"No. We're done here. I'm just waiting for Josef to grab those two stray cats he trapped by the dumpster. We're going to drop them off at the shelter on our way home."

Clara walked slowly to the coat rack by the door.

"What are you planning to do this evening?" Maisie asked.

Clara shrugged. "Unless the TV reception in my room has improved, I'll be watching baking shows on my laptop. Same as every other night. I guess that's why I got the bee in my bonnet about homemade puff pastry."

Maisie chuckled. "I love those shows. We've watched them all multiple times. I've gotten some great ideas from them."

"What are you doing tonight?" Clara reciprocated.

"I'm going to choir practice," Maisie said. "We're singing Handel's *Messiah* on the Sunday before Christmas."

"That's one of my favorites," Clara said. "I sang it with the choir in college."

Maisie put her index finger along her cheek. "Why don't you join me at practice tonight? You have a lovely voice."

"I'm not going to be here the Sunday before Christmas, Maisie."

"That won't matter. This isn't just for our choir. Members of the community can join in, too. There are no tryouts and everyone's welcome. You already know and love the music—you said so yourself. I'll bet you'd enjoy singing with us tonight."

Clara paused on her way to the door.

"Lots of people rehearse who never turn up for the performance. You've been stuck in that motel room every night since your car broke down. It's high time you got out."

Clara's shoulders relaxed, and she smiled at Maisie. "I am getting a little stir crazy in there," she replied. "If you're sure I won't be in the way."

"I'm positive."

"Then I'd love to."

"Great! Practice goes from seven until nine. Josef and I will pick you up at six forty."

"I'll be waiting outside the motel lobby," Clara said. "And thank you."

Josef pulled his car to a stop at the walkway to the sanctuary. "I'll be right here at nine," he said. "You gals have fun."

"We will," Maisie said. "This is my favorite piece of music," she said to Clara as they got out of the car. "Our choir only has twenty-five members, but with singers from the community and other church choirs joining us, we'll have a hundred voices—maybe more."

"Wow. It's always fun to sing with a large group," Clara replied.

They made their way to the cluster of people milling around the entrance, waiting for the doors to be unlocked.

"We rehearse in the sanctuary because our choir room won't hold this many people." Maisie approached a circle of young women, chatting amiably. "Let me introduce you."

Clara hung back. "I'm only coming to one practice. There's no need …"

Maisie took Clara's elbow and pulled her toward the women. "Hello, everybody."

"Maisie!" cried one of the women as they all turned to her. "I'm so glad you're singing with us."

"You look terrific," replied another woman. "How are you?"

"I'm doing well. The doctors tell me I'll be right as rain in another couple of months. I've got a friend with me that I'd like you to meet."

All eyes shifted to Clara.

"This is Clara Conway. She's new in town and helping Josef and me at the diner. I heard her singing in the bakery—she's got a beautiful first soprano—and I persuaded her to join us."

"That's great, Clara. I sing that part, too, and we can use some additional support."

"Welcome to Pinewood," said another woman. "You're going to love it here."

"Thank you, but I'm … I'm not staying," Clara said. "I'm only here temporarily—I'll be leaving next week."

Another woman opened her mouth to comment when the locks clicked, and the heavy mahogany doors swung open.

The singers streamed into the narthex. A tall man motioned them toward the sanctuary, where chairs had been arranged in a semicircle on risers placed in the chancel. "Take a seat in your section," he advised. "You know what part you sing."

"I'm an alto," Maisie said to Clara when they reached the seats. "I'll meet you out front when we're done." She glanced at Clara, who was sweeping her gaze around the church. "It's beautiful, isn't it?"

"It most certainly is," Clara replied in hushed tones. "The wooden beams are lovely, and that three-story stained-glass window is spectacular."

"It faces west. You should see it during the daytime, when the sun's streaming through it."

"I'll bet it's breathtaking."

Maisie beamed. "It's not ornate or fancy, but we're proud of it."

"I can see why. There's a timeless, welcoming feel to this space."

"Enjoy yourself tonight, dear," Maisie said, patting Clara's arm before she secured a seat in the alto section.

Clara inhaled deeply and selected a chair in the back row of first sopranos. How long had it been since she'd sat in church? She honestly couldn't remember. She turned her attention to the group of singers, exchanging hugs and pleasantries as they filed into place. Clara had been the girl who'd won Sunday school attendance awards. Why had she allowed this to slip out of her life?

The tall man from the narthex stepped to a music stand in the open center of the semi-circle. He picked up a baton and tapped on the stand.

Conversations stopped abruptly and all eyes turned to him.

The man nodded to four people positioned at either end of the semi-circle. They each carried tall stacks of musical scores and began passing them along the rows.

"Take one and hand the rest along," the choir director said. "We'll collect them at the end of rehearsal. We're going to start with 'For Unto Us, A Child is Born.' Find your place, please."

He waited as the choir flipped pages.

"We're going to be accompanied on the organ in our rehearsals by our own Kurt Holbrook."

He swung his arm to the back of the church and an ornately carved organ, flanked by an impressive array of pipes.

Clara's eyes opened wide. Kurt stood and waved to the choir from behind the organ.

Clara shook her head in disbelief. Kurt was a Renaissance man, if there ever was one.

The choir director once more tapped his music stand and gestured to Kurt. The familiar strains of Handel's masterpiece filled the room.

Clara took a deep breath, glanced at the music in her hands, and began to sing. She could hardly believe that two hours had gone by when the choir director told them to pass their scores to the end of the row, where the same people waited to collect them.

"There's a sign-up sheet in the narthex for choir robes," he said. "We're borrowing robes from other churches so that everyone can have one. Just put down your name, the part you sing, and your size. We'll be rehearsing on Tuesdays and Thursdays, from seven until nine, until the performance."

He took a deep breath before he concluded. "Thank you all for coming tonight. We've made great progress. See you next time."

The choir filed out of the sanctuary quickly. The casual chatter that filled the air before rehearsal started wasn't renewed.

It's a work night, Clara surmised as she made her way out of the church. She paused by the sign-up table for choir robes, then proceeded to the exit. She would be long gone by the Sunday before Christmas. She turned to find Maisie and didn't have far to look. Kurt had taken her elbow and was escorting her to Josef's car, idling at the end of the walkway.

Clara wove her way through the people heading to the parking lot.

"There she is," Clara heard Maisie say.

Kurt turned around. "Hello," he said.

"Hi," Clara replied.

Kurt opened the rear car door for her.

"You are a man of many talents," she said. "You did a great job tonight. I play piano and have a good idea of how hard that was."

"Thank you," he said. "I almost pursued a career as a classical musician."

Clara lowered herself into her seat. "Really? I'd like to know more."

Kurt shrugged and closed the door, tapping on the roof of the car before Josef pulled away.

Chapter 12

Clara leaned her elbows on the counter and stared into the depths of her second cup of coffee. It was the middle of the afternoon on Tuesday. She was finishing her lunch, which she had started taking after the noon rush subsided. She stabbed the last morsel of brownie with her fork, being careful to swirl it in the drizzle of salted caramel sauce that remained on her plate and popped it into her mouth. It took an act of will power to prevent herself from moaning in pleasure. It was a good thing that her car would be fixed on Thursday. She hadn't stepped on a scale since she'd arrived in Pinewood, and she didn't want to. The only exercise she got was walking between the motel and the diner, and she'd been sampling everything that came out of the bakery—as a matter of professional interest—she'd told herself.

Someone tapped her on the shoulder, and she spun around on the counter stool to find Kurt looking at her now-empty plate.

"Is that one of Maisie's brownies?"

Clara covered her mouth with her hand and nodded, chewing the sticky, chocolatey goodness.

"That's my favorite thing she makes. Those hazelnut things last week are a close second."

Clara smiled but kept her mouth shut. She was sure she had chocolate smeared all over her teeth.

"I hope that wasn't the last one?"

Clara took a long swig of her coffee. "Let me go find out. You want one?"

"For sure. And I need to order lunch. I doubt I'll get away from the office in time for dinner before choir practice tonight."

Clara stood and walked to the other side of the counter while Kurt removed his topcoat, revealing a tailored blue suit, white shirt, and gray-striped tie. "I spent the morning in court," he told Clara.

"You look very … formidable," she said.

Kurt laughed. "I guess that's a good thing."

"In your line of work? It most certainly is." Clara held up a coffee cup, and Kurt nodded. She filled it and placed it on the counter in front of him. "Do you know what you'd like to eat? Besides that brownie?"

"I didn't get breakfast, either. I'm starved. How about the meatloaf plate with sides of mashed potatoes and green beans?"

"That should hold you until after choir practice," Clara said. "I'll put your order in and bring you that brownie—so you know you've got it."

"I like the way you think," he replied.

Clara disappeared behind the swinging door into the kitchen and returned with an extra-large brownie, drizzled in caramel sauce. She placed it on the counter and reached for the pot to refill his coffee.

"You're a very talented organist," Clara said. "You must have studied for a long time. That level of skill doesn't just happen."

"Thank you," Kurt said. "I majored in organ performance as an undergraduate. I had grand dreams of playing in one of the major cathedrals in Europe."

"What happened? I'll bet you were good enough."

"I might have been, if I'd continued my studies and gotten my Ph.D. I studied abroad during my junior year and realized how many talented people—more talented than me—were chasing the same dream. I also learned that my chosen path wasn't likely to be a lucrative one."

Clara nodded. "That's a common theme for creative types. How'd you settle on the law?"

"I was on the debate team in high school and loved it. One of my college advisors suggested I look into law school. I took the LSAT on a whim—as a walk in—and scored well. I applied to law school, and the rest, as they say, is history."

"Do you enjoy being a lawyer?"

"Very much. It's been a good career for me."

"You don't regret not pursuing your interest in music?"

"Not at all. I get to use my skills a couple times a year at things like this *Messiah* concert. That keeps my hand in and—frankly—I don't have time for more."

A bell rang from the kitchen behind her, signaling that Kurt's order was up.

Clara removed the plate from under the warming lights and set it in front of him.

"Will we see you at choir practice this week?"

"Well … my car should be ready on Thursday. I plan to move on as soon as I get it back, so I won't be here for the Thursday night rehearsal."

Kurt directed his attention to his plate. "Well, then, come one last time."

"I promised Maisie I would. She and Josef are picking me up tonight."

"I'll drive the two of you home afterward," Kurt said. "Tell Josef that he won't have to come back for you."

"That's awfully nice." Clara smoothed her apron and straightened the collar of her shirt. She removed the dirty dishes from the counter in front of him and slid the brownie into their place. "Do you have room for a scoop of ice cream with that?"

He flashed her a grin. "Why not?"

"If you're only eating one meal a day, may as well make it count."

"Exactly."

Clara emerged from the kitchen with a large scoop of homemade vanilla ice cream. "I'll see you later," she said, setting it next to his brownie.

Kurt nodded, giving the brownie and ice cream his full attention.

Chapter 13

"Sorry this took so long," Andy said, holding the key fob and a credit card receipt out to Clara.

"It wasn't your fault that they sent the wrong part." She folded the receipt into thirds and tucked it into a pocket in her wallet.

"I hope you've enjoyed your time in Pinewood," he said. "I hear you were indispensable at the diner—they couldn't have managed the Thanksgiving pies without you."

"I had the time of my life, actually," Clara said. "In a strange way, this felt like exactly what I needed."

"Life's like that. You can make all the plans in the world, but sometimes fate plops you down right where you're meant to be." He nodded. "Maisie and Josef loved having you there."

"They're about the kindest people I've ever met," Clara replied. "I'll never forget them."

"Where is it you said you were headed when your car broke down?"

"I don't have a fixed destination in mind."

Andy pursed his lips. "Well … have a safe trip—wherever you're going."

"Thank you. I'd better grab my stuff from the motel and hit the road."

"Are you heading east? There's a blizzard coming that way later tonight."

"I hadn't heard that."

"It's supposed to miss us. If you set out to the west, you should be fine."

"That's my plan. Thank you for everything."

They shook hands, and she walked to her car. She'd return her attorney's call, check out of her motel room, and take off. She'd said another goodbye to Maisie and Josef yesterday afternoon before they'd departed for the day and couldn't bear to see the disappointment on their faces again.

Clara placed the call to her attorney as she entered her motel room.

"Mr. Gilbert is available. Let me put you through," said the receptionist.

"Clara," came the booming voice on the other end of the line. "How are you?"

"Fine, thank you." She held her phone to her ear with one hand while she picked up her bag of toiletries and began taking it out to her car.

"Have you settled somewhere? Do you have a forwarding address?"

"Not yet, Tom," Clara said. "It's a long story. I'm still on the road." His voice message had sounded ominous. He'd said there would be a delay in her proceedings. She wanted him to get to the point of this call. "You said you served Travis but that things might not move along as quickly as we'd hoped. When we talked before, you said that I was being more than generous with the property division—that Travis would have nothing to fight about. Has something changed?"

"He can't object to the terms you've proposed—you're letting him have all of the property acquired during the marriage—despite my advice to the contrary."

"I don't need anything that we had," Clara said. "I just want to close this chapter of my life and move on."

"Understood. That's what you said."

"So what's up?"

"He's hired an attorney and they've filed papers disputing your mental state."

"WHAT?!"

"They're saying that you're not mentally competent—that your running away is evidence of that."

"Oh, for—" Clara sputtered, choking back the curse on her lips. "That's ridiculous. Anyone who *wouldn't* divorce a cheating asshole of a husband like mine would have to be insane."

"I don't want you to worry about this. We can handle it. I'm talking to his attorney tomorrow, and I'll file a response with the court. I needed to advise you of this development."

Clara reached her car and paused, setting her bag on the pavement. She put her arm on the roof of the car and leaned her forehead against it. "I can't believe he's pulling this stunt."

"I understand he was furious when he was served."

Clara inhaled slowly. She felt a tiny surge of pleasure that Travis had been the one to be upset, for once in their marriage.

"You don't need to be concerned," Tom said. "People make all sorts of unfounded accusations in divorce actions. I'll sort it out."

"Okay," she said quietly.

"Be sure to let me know when you get settled," he said and disconnected the call.

Clara lifted her eyes to the horizon, where the sun had almost set, and the sky was heavy with dark clouds. She suddenly didn't want to be alone in her car, heading out in the dark to a new roadside motel in an unfamiliar destination. Her mind would replay the call with her attorney on a continuous loop. Travis's ridiculous allegations would only make her miserable.

She picked up the bag and marched back into her motel room. She wanted to be around people, wanted to be immersed in the goodness of a group working toward a common goal. She wanted to be at choir practice.

She got in her car and easily found her way to the church. Clara walked into the sanctuary and slipped into her section as they were getting started.

She glanced at Maisie and was relieved to see that the older woman had not seen her come in. Clara would leave rehearsal as soon as they were done, get a good night's sleep, and head out of Pinewood early the next morning.

Chapter 14

Clara opened one eye and swung her hand to her nightstand, groping for her phone. She twisted the screen to her face. She still had another half hour before her alarm was set to go off. She pushed her head back into her pillow and squeezed her eyes shut. Instead of drifting back to sleep, her mind returned to last night's conversation with her attorney.

She swung her legs over the side of her bed and padded across the carpeted floor to stand at the window. A draft of frigid air from the window casing swirled around her feet. She placed one foot on top of the other and curled her toes together in a futile attempt to keep them warm.

Clara parted the curtains to look out at the day before her. She wasn't expecting the sight that met her eyes.

The parking lot was blanketed with an unblemished covering of snow. Large, wet flakes swirled to the ground. The rising sun fought, unsuccessfully, with the heavy clouds hugging the horizon.

Clara tugged the curtain back into place and crossed to the television. The local news channel confirmed what she had seen—the blizzard had veered to the west and Pinewood had caught the brunt of it. Seven inches had fallen overnight, and another ten inches were expected before early evening, when the storm was predicted to abate.

Clara sat on the bed and flopped onto her back. She certainly wasn't going to be driving anywhere today. She turned to crawl under the covers when she stopped suddenly. She knew what she needed to do.

Clara took a quick shower and moved purposely around the room, getting herself dressed. She parted the curtains again and glanced at the diner. The front parking lot was empty. She couldn't see the lot in back. The neon "OPEN" sign above the entrance was dark. As she stared, it blinked twice and then remained on, casting pink and blue ribbons of light in the snow.

Someone had opened the diner. Whether it was Josef or one of the others, they were bound to be shorthanded today, with cooks or servers being snowed in. She could help with that.

Clara put on her jogging shoes and forced her way to her car through snow that came past her ankle. She rummaged in her belongings and finally located her winter boots. She changed footwear in the front seat, stashed her jogging shoes, and headed across the parking lot.

The aroma of freshly brewed coffee greeted her when she opened the door. Two of the morning-shift cooks and one waitress were milling about, tending to their duties.

One of the cooks spied her and raised a hand in greeting. "I thought you left yesterday."

"That was my plan," Clara said with a rue smile, "but I didn't get out of Dodge in time. I came over to see if you need any help."

"Josef and Maisie can't get in until their street and driveway are plowed. It's gonna be just the three of us," he said, gesturing to his co-workers. "We won't be busy today, so we'll be fine."

"Except that we're supplying fifty dozen Christmas cookies for refreshments after the *Messiah* concert on Sunday," the waitress said. "None of the bakers can get here today, and the roads may not be clear enough by tomorrow."

"They can live without cookies," the other cook said.

"It's tradition," the waitress said, giving him a sidelong glance.

"I can bake the cookies," Clara said.

"Really?" asked the first cook.

"You can make fifty dozen. All by yourself?" the other cook said, raising an eyebrow at her.

"Absolutely. No problem," Clara heard herself say, wondering if that were true.

"The keys to the bakery are on the hook by the back door," said the cook. "Do you want to call Maisie for the recipe?"

Clara paused on her way across the kitchen. "Why don't we keep this our secret? A surprise for Maisie."

A smile spread across the waitress's face. "I love surprises. She thinks the church is going to have to serve packaged cookies from the grocery. She'll be thrilled to see that the diner's pulled through once again."

"It's settled, then," Clara said.

"Is there anything you need from us?"

"Just a large carafe of coffee, if you don't mind. And maybe send over a sandwich at lunchtime. I'm going to be very busy."

"You've got it," the cook said. "I'll brew some fresh and bring it over."

"Thank you," Clara said, lifting the keys from the ring and heading into the snow. She had her mother's cookie cutters and her sugar cookie recipe, which she'd committed to memory and knew how to scale it up to commercial quantities. Her mind was already racing with the shapes she'd bake and the decorations she'd apply. She'd glimpsed a plastic tub labeled 'Pastry Bags and Tips' on a high shelf in the bakery. If it held what she needed, Clara would make Maisie proud.

Chapter 15

Clara placed a sheet of bakery paper over the last layer of baked snowflakes, each traced in a thin line of icing accented with silver nonpareils and dusted with iridescent sugar. With the angels, ornaments, stars, and wreaths, all exquisitely iced in careful detail, Johanson's was providing an array fit for a five-star hotel. She placed a piece of tape on each side of the rectangular pink bakery box.

The plastic tub of pastry supplies had contained every tool she required to turn out these exquisite cookies in large numbers. The inventory of flour, sugar, vanilla, shortening, and salt had been more than enough for Clara to turn out the sixty-five dozen cookies that now sat in boxes, waiting to be transported to the church. Working alone in the quiet bakery, enveloped in the rich aromas of vanilla and baking cookies, was a balm to Clara's battered soul.

After the bluster and cold of the past two days, Sunday had dawned mild and sunny. The roads were finally clear, and Clara anticipated that the sanctuary would be filled to its three-hundred-fifty-person capacity. With the one-hundred-person choir and the ushers, sound and lighting technicians, and the orchestra, they would easily need the extra fifteen dozen. She had even bagged up a cookie for each choir member, together with a dozen for Kurt as a thank you for accompanying them during rehearsals.

Clara checked her watch. It was time. She would get all of these displayed long before the choir arrived. She'd slip into the back of the sanctuary to watch the performance, then hurry to the hall where the reception was being held after the concert. Clara wanted to see Maisie's face when she saw what Clara had worked so hard to produce.

Clara's was the fourth car in the parking lot. She located the hall where the reception was to be held, but the doors were locked. She headed for the sanctuary, hoping to run into the choir director or a custodian. She opened the heavy outer door and found herself face-to-face with Kurt.

"Clara? Did you … did you come back for the concert?"

Clara shook her head. "I never left—I got snowed in."

"Josef and Maisie didn't tell me."

"They don't know I'm still here," Maisie said, unable to suppress her grin. "I have a surprise for them, but I need someone to unlock the reception hall for me."

Kurt turned to a man adjusting the lighting in the narthex. "Can you let me have the key to fellowship hall?"

The man handed him a ring of keys.

"What's this surprise you're so pleased about?" Kurt and Clara began walking.

"It's not that big a deal, really." Clara shrugged. "Maisie and Josef couldn't get to the diner over the weekend, so I made the Christmas cookies for the reception after the performance. We decided to keep it a secret from them. They think the church went out and bought cookies at the grocery."

Kurt gave her a sidelong glance as he unlocked the door. "Do you need any help bringing them in?"

"I can get it," Clara said. "I also made a dozen for you—to thank you for helping us at rehearsal."

They had reached her car and she opened the trunk. She removed a small pink box, tied with white satin ribbon, and handed it to him.

"Thank you," Kurt said. "I've got quite a sweet tooth and I'm starved. Can I have one right now?"

"Sure. They're yours—no strings attached."

Kurt untied the ribbon and opened the lid. He froze, his hand halfway to a cookie. "You made these?"

Clara nodded. A flush began to rise from her collar.

"I've never seen anything like them. They're … works of art. They sure smell good, too."

"Thank you. Let's see how they taste."

"I've always thought this is one of the stupidest sayings in the world, but they're too pretty to eat."

"I sure hope you're wrong," Clara said, smiling broadly, "because I made sixty-five dozen. That's a lot of cookies to not eat."

"You're kidding me, right?"

She shook her head. "Cookies just like those are in all of these boxes." She swept her arm across the pink bakery boxes stacked in her car.

"People will be talking about this for years," Kurt said. "You're going to be a legend in Pinewood."

"You think Maisie will be pleased?"

"I think pleased won't begin to describe it," Kurt said. "I'll bet she'll start crying and won't stop."

Clara turned to her car and stacked three boxes to carry inside. "I'm not sure that's what I'm going for, but I do hope she'll be proud of them."

"I'll help you get these inside," Kurt said. "You'll want to be done in time to warm up with the choir."

"I'm not singing," Clara said. "I didn't sign up for a choir robe, and I didn't attend the dress rehearsal over the weekend. I plan to slip in the back and listen to the performance."

"I can find you a choir robe," Kurt said. "The dress rehearsal got cancelled due to the snow. You're as ready as anyone. Maisie told me what a good voice you have." He faced her. "Wouldn't you like to sing with the choir?"

"Well … yes, I would."

"I'll help you get these out of the car. I'm assuming you've got some fancy display in mind?"

Clara nodded.

"You set that up, and I'll find you a robe."

"I don't want Maisie to know I'm here until after the performance."

"I'll bring it back here. You can warm up on your own."

"I will. Scout's honor." Clara made the Girl Scout sign.

Kurt laughed. "This is going to make Maisie's day. I can't wait to see her face."

Kurt and Clara exchanged a conspiratorial smile and began shuttling the cookies to the reception hall.

The majestic concluding strains of the "Hallelujah" chorus hung in the air. The audience, already on its feet, burst into applause. The choir director rested his baton on the music stand. Cries of "bravo" and whistles erupted from behind him. He turned to the audience and spread his arms to include the soloists on either side of him before gesturing to the orchestra and choir behind him.

The audience response rose in intensity.

Clara blinked back tears. She'd experienced the same intense emotional reaction when she'd sung the *Messiah* in college. She gazed out at the audience. Late afternoon sun streamed through the arched stained-glass windows, painting the sanctuary in jewel tones. Clara promised herself she would join a church choir in her new hometown. She hoped she would find a church like this.

The applause finally died down and the audience began to file out of the sanctuary in an orderly fashion.

Clara made her way to the aisle, murmuring "excuse me" and "sorry" as she hurried past her fellow sopranos who were gathering their music and exchanging remarks with their neighbors. She wanted to make sure she was in place, by the refreshment table, when Maisie got there.

She skirted clusters of people chatting amiably in the mild afternoon and entered the reception hall. Three women stood in front of the table displaying her cookies. One was pointing to the table while another brought her hand to her heart.

Clara moved closer and heard the third woman say, "I've never seen more beautiful cookies in my life! Not even in a magazine."

Clara's pulse raced.

"I couldn't agree more," replied the woman who had been pointing. "Maisie's outdone herself." She picked up a cookie in the shape of an ornament.

"I'm going to get a picture of these, before they're all gone," said the third woman, bringing her camera up and snapping photos. "I'm going to send these pictures to my daughter. She and my grandchildren love to bake sugar cookies."

Clara claimed a spot behind the table and off to one side. She watched as people began to surge toward the table, exclaiming over her beautiful creations.

The cookies began to go fast as word travelled around the room about the exquisite treats.

Clara rose on her tiptoes, searching for Maisie. If she didn't get here soon, there wouldn't be any left for her to see. She was wondering if she should go in search of her friend when two men in front of the table stepped back and made way for Maisie and Josef.

Clara locked her gaze on Maisie's face. She wasn't disappointed in Maisie's reaction.

The older woman's eyes grew wide and she brought her hand to her forehead. She swiveled her face to Josef.

He shrugged.

Maisie turned back to the cookies and leaned over the table, taking her time to examine each of the intricately decorated shapes. "Where in the world?" she began as she raised her eyes and caught sight of Clara. She blinked and then held out her arms to the young woman.

Clara moved around the table to Maisie, who threw her arms around her. "You. Did. This." she whispered in Clara's hair.

Clara nodded.

Maisie leaned back and her eyes were shining. "These are masterpieces, dear. I don't have the skill or vision to pull this off."

"I'm so pleased you like them," Clara said.

Josef leaned into them. "I think you're holding up the line, ladies. Take a cookie and step aside." He gestured behind him. "I think we're holding up the line."

"Good idea," Clara said.

Maisie selected an angel, and Josef reached for a snowflake. The three of them moved to one side.

"I've got a dozen, boxed up for you, back at the diner," Clara said.

Josef took a bite of his cookie and moaned. "They taste even better than they look."

Clara grinned.

"I thought that you'd left town," Maisie said. "What happened?"

"I got snowed in," Clara said. "I went to the diner on Friday morning to see if you needed help. When I learned that you couldn't make it to the bakery and Johanson's wouldn't be able to supply Christmas cookies—breaking a centuries-old tradition," she embellished, "I knew I had to stay and prevent that from happening."

"Why didn't anyone tell us?" Maisie asked. "I almost didn't come in here to see these. I was so disappointed about letting everyone down that Josef and I were heading to our car as soon as we left the sanctuary."

"I was becoming increasingly nervous that you weren't going to show up," Clara said. "What changed your mind?"

"Kurt," Josef said. "He caught us and insisted. He said that people wanted to see us and knew that we'd been snowed in."

"Told us to get over ourselves!" Maisie said, smiling.

"I'm so glad he did," Clara said. "I know it's silly, but I was excited about surprising you."

"It's wonderful," Maisie said, removing her glasses and swiping a hand across her eyes. "These are beautiful, and I'm touched that you went to so much trouble."

"Of course, I would," Clara said, her voice thick with emotion. "I don't think anyone's shown me more kindness. I was thrilled that there was something nice I could do for you."

"You know what the best part of all this is?" Maisie asked.

Clara raised her eyebrows and shrugged.

"You're here." She leaned in and put her arm around Clara's shoulder. "I was missing you already."

"Now that you're still here," Josef said, "I think you'll have to stay and spend Christmas with us."

"He's right." Maisie seized on the suggestion with gusto. "You can't go searching for a new home the week before Christmas."

"Another storm is headed our way, too," Josef said. "You wouldn't want to be out on the road and get stranded—again. There aren't many places as nice as Pinewood."

Clara laughed. "You mean as welcoming as the owners of Johanson's Diner." She grew serious. "I think you're right. I don't want to be a stranger in a strange town on Christmas. If it's not an imposition, I'd love to stay—through Christmas."

Maisie clapped her hands together. "Perfect!"

"Can I help out at the bakery? Will you be busy?"

"We always are. And once word gets around town about these cookies," Maisie held up hers as if she were raising a glass to make a toast, "we'll have customers placing orders by the dozen."

"That'll be fine by me," Clara said. "I've got them down to a science."

"Maybe you can teach me how to make that puff pastry that people are still talking about," Maisie said.

"I'd love to," Clara said.

The two women smiled into each other's eyes, both thinking that the upcoming week might be the happiest they'd each had in a very long time.

Chapter 16

Maisie sank into her chair in the bakery workroom, letting out a heavy sigh. She glanced at the window, where heavy clouds portended an early dusk. The clock above the door showed it was almost three thirty.

"It feels later than it is." She covered a yawn with her hand.

Clara sprayed disinfectant on the long worktable and began wiping. "There's only a handful of orders remaining to be picked up. Why don't you and Josef head home?"

"That's a good idea. Josef should be ready to go soon. We close the diner at two on Christmas Eve afternoon and we're not open on Christmas Day." She yawned again. "I'm really bushed."

"It's no wonder," Clara said. "We never should have accepted orders for ninety dozen cookies and offered up a white chocolate raspberry tart on puff pastry in the diner. It was just too much."

"Maybe, but it sure was fun making all that." Maisie's eyes twinkled. "Before my stroke, it wouldn't have fazed me."

"You need to go home and get a nap."

"I think you're right." Maisie began to rise and swayed unsteadily. She sat down again quickly.

Clara dropped the rag and came to her side. "Are you all right?"

"Just a bit dizzy, is all."

Clara bent over and peered into Maisie's face.

"It's nothing," Maisie said. "Happens when I overdo."

"I'll get Josef. You're going home."

"Thank you, dear. Don't alarm him. I don't need him fussing over me."

Clara snatched her jacket from the hook by the door and threw it over her shoulders before jogging to the back door of the diner.

She stepped inside and found the kitchen deserted, counters clean and the commercial dishwasher humming. "Josef," she called, crossing through to the dining room, which was also empty.

She retraced her steps and exited the diner in time to see Josef on his hands and knees by the dumpster, holding out a tasty morsel and cooing softly to a creature she couldn't see.

Clara began walking toward him, the heels of her boots making a clacking sound. Josef turned his head in her direction and held up a hand to stop her.

Clara stood still and waited.

A small, furry head with a black nose and enormous dark eyes came into view as the creature stretched its mouth toward the proffered treat.

Josef slowly moved the treat farther back, and the dog inched its way forward. He finally allowed the dog to take the morsel while at the same time bringing his other hand around to grasp the animal firmly behind its shoulders.

The small dog attempted to wriggle its way free, but Josef brought it to his chest and held it firm. The dog stopped squirming and stayed rigidly still. Josef began to rub between the dog's ears as he made his way to Clara.

"Look at this little gal," Josef said. "Good girl," he crooned. "She's been hanging out by the dumpster all week. Nobody's going to be here until day after tomorrow. I couldn't bear to leave her here, out in the cold, on her own. Not at Christmas. I'll drop her off at the no-kill shelter."

The dog turned her muzzle, matted with dirt and full of nettles, into Josef's chest.

"She seems like a sweet little thing, doesn't she?" he asked.

Clara reached out a hand to touch her. The dog turned her head to Clara and licked her, wagging her tail.

"You're a friendly sort, aren't you?" Josef said to the dog. He glanced back at Clara and stiffened, taking in her serious expression. "Is something wrong?"

"No … nothing's wrong, but Maisie seems very tired to me. She had a bit of a dizzy spell, just now."

Josef quickened his pace to his car. "I'll put this girl in my carrier, and then I'll get Maisie and take her home."

"I think that's a good idea. She says she needs a nap." Clara walked alongside him. "Why don't I drop this gal off at the shelter? We've only got a handful of bakery orders remaining to be picked up. I can wait for those customers, lock up, and then run her to the shelter."

Josef secured the dog in the carrier.

"You're sure? I'd like to get Maisie home as soon as possible."

"Positive." Clara reached into the car and pulled out the carrier. "I'll bring her into the bakery with me and drop her off as soon as the last order is picked up."

"She really shouldn't be in there," Josef said.

"I'll hide her in the office," Clara said. "As far as you know, I kept her outside."

Josef hesitated.

"It's Christmas Eve. It'll be fine. I should only be here another half hour. People know they need to pick up by four."

"Okay. Thanks," Josef said. He opened his driver's side door and began searching in the console for paper and pen. "I'll write down the address for you."

Clara peered into the carrier at the dog who was now huddled in the back corner. Her wavy coat appeared to be brown and white under the thick blanket of mud. She had a long body and short legs. Terrier with a dash of dachshund, Clara surmised. Her eyes were bright, and her nose twitched rapidly as she tried to get Clara's scent. She'd be an attractive dog when she was cleaned up, Clara thought. Too bad she hadn't been collected earlier. She might have ended up under someone's Christmas tree—might have found her forever home.

Clara was startled out of her reverie as Josef pressed the paper with the shelter's address into her hand.

"I really appreciate this," he reiterated, as they walked toward the bakery. "We'll see you tomorrow—dinner's at four."

"Why don't we cancel that?" Clara said. "You and Maisie don't need company. It's been so busy—ever since Thanksgiving. You should rest."

"Nonsense. We've both been looking forward to having you over. Maisie's sister will be there, and she does all the cooking. We don't lift a finger, and there'll be plenty."

"You're sure?"

Josef nodded.

"Then I'll be there. What can I bring?"

"Just yourself," Josef said. "Why don't the two of you wait around the corner while I get Maisie to the car?"

Clara tucked the carrier under her arm and cocked her head to one side.

"I'm pretty sure Maisie won't want our new friend, here," he pointed to the carrier, "inside the bakery."

"Gotcha," Clara said, heading to the side of the bakery. "Good thinking." She stepped out of sight, calling over her shoulder, "Merry Christmas!"

Chapter 17

Clara took the woman's elbow and turned her toward the door. "No worries. I was happy to stay."

"It's just that my mother's been talking about these nonstop since last Sunday and I promised to bring them for dinner tomorrow."

"We're delighted to hear that," Clara said, grasping the door handle.

"I'm sorry I was so late. I'm glad that you waited for me."

"It's a good thing you called," Clara said. "I was locking up when I heard the phone ringing and came back inside to answer it." She pulled the door open.

"I know I said I'd be here in five minutes," the woman said, moving slowly to the door. "I couldn't believe that I ran into road construction. Why in the world are they tearing up the streets on Christmas Eve? That cost me another twenty minutes. Honestly ..."

Clara made a point of checking the time on her phone.

"You probably have somewhere you need to be," the woman said, stepping out into the growing dusk.

"I have a delivery. Before five," Clara said. She looked up at the woman and forced a smile. "Merry Christmas," she said, closing the door on the woman and securing the lock.

Clara ran across the bakery, shoving her arms into her jacket, and snatched her purse off of the desk in the office. She hoisted the dog carrier and made her way swiftly out the rear door of the bakery.

Josef had said that the shelter was twenty minutes away and it would be open until five. Clara hoped they hadn't closed early on Christmas Eve. She should make it there in the nick of time.

She had checked on the dog while she'd been waiting for customers to pick up their orders. She'd fed her the generous heel of a loaf of bread, which she'd gulped down in chunks so large that she'd made herself cough and hack.

Clara had filled a saucer with water and placed it inside the door to the carrier. The dog had taken a long, noisy drink, then circled twice and settled down for a nap. Clara had stared at her face—her eyes slits—as her chest rose and fell with her rhythmic breathing. *I'll bet this is the first warm place you've been in for quite a while.* She hoped the poor creature felt safe and secure.

The dog began to whimper as she pulled onto the road running past the diner and turned in the opposite direction of the motel.

"You're okay," Clara said in sing-song tones. "You're going to a place where you'll be warm, and they'll feed you every day. Pretty soon someone will take you home and love you." She rested her hand on top of the carrier on the seat next to her.

She was making good time on her journey until her route took her past St. Thomas the Apostle Church. Cars were backed up in both directions. Traffic inched along.

Clara noted the large sign that announced the Family Christmas Eve Service at five o'clock.

She sucked in a breath and checked the clock on her dashboard. She'd really be cutting it close.

The traffic finally cleared, and she pulled up to the animal shelter in time to see the taillights of a pickup truck driving away. The inside lights were out. She parked at the entrance and left her car running as she sprinted to the door and grasped the handle.

Clara pulled but the door was locked. She rapped on the metal frame with her knuckles and called, "Hello—anybody there?" already knowing that there was not.

She sighed heavily and brought her hand to her head, brushing her hair off of her face. Now what? She was staying at a motel—that didn't allow dogs.

She returned to her car and shut the door with a solid *thwack*.

The dog was now on her feet and came to the grate, sticking her nose through the wires.

"What am I going to do with you?"

Her tail began to move slowly back and forth.

"Should I take you to Josef?" Clara reached over and stuck her fingers through the grate to scratch her nose.

The dog licked her fingertips. Her tail began to wag furiously.

"I'd take you back to the diner, but I don't have a key." She bent down and put her face to the grate. "I guess you're stuck with me, for tonight only. Or tonight and tomorrow. Until the shelter opens again. That's all."

The dog let out a short "Woof."

"Shhh . . ." Clara admonished. "There'll be none of that. No one at the motel can know that I have a dog in my room."

The dog lowered her head to her front paws, her back side in the air. Her tail wagged even faster.

"Here's our plan," Clara addressed the dog. "We'll stop at a convenience store to get dog food and a collar and leash, if they have them. You can stay with me, but you'll have to be very quiet."

The dog looked up at Clara and held perfectly still. Clara thought she understood.

"You'll have to go to the door when you need to go out. No peeing or pooping in my room!"

The tail wagging resumed.

"I'll hide you under my jacket and take you over to the grassy area in front of the diner to do your business." She put her face close to the grate. "Understand?"

The dog settled onto her stomach.

"Okay, then. Let's do this thing," Clara said, steering onto the road.

She stopped at the first convenience store she passed. She bought the necessary kibble and a pink collar with daisies running down the center and a matching leash. She also grabbed a box of treats, a sleeve of tennis balls, and a plush dog toy, in the shape of a gingerbread man, with a squeaker. While she waited in line at the register, she put a package of almonds and a bag of string cheese into her basket. She'd need something for her own dinner.

She returned to her car to find the dog waiting, alert and quiet, in the carrier.

Clara stopped at the diner and dug the collar and leash out of the shopping bag. The dog accepted these without objection.

The dog dutifully did her business on command and hopped back into the car.

"You belonged to someone once upon a time, didn't you?" Clara asked as the dog voluntarily stepped back into the carrier. "I think you're well trained. Someone must be missing you. Are you sad without your people?" She looked into the dog's eyes. "You don't look sad."

The dog wagged her tail.

The motel was quiet, and Clara encountered no one as she hurried to her room with her furry charge under her jacket and the bags full of dog supplies on her arm.

Clara had dreaded spending Christmas Eve alone. She smiled to herself. She'd never thought that she'd spend it with a rescue dog. What was the old saying? Be careful what you wish for?

She took a towel from the bathroom, laid it on the floor, and spread a handful of kibble on it.

The dog moved to the towel and downed it in under a minute, doing her best to lick every crumb from the towel.

Clara looked around for something to use as a water bowl. She wished she hadn't left the saucer back at the bakery. Her foundation makeup had a large, round cap. It would have to do. She removed the cap, washed it thoroughly in the sink, and filled it with fresh water.

The dog watched her carefully, as if knowing what she was going to do.

Clara set the makeshift water bowl next to the washcloth.

The dog lapped gratefully.

Clara clicked on the television and stretched out on the bed to eat her convenience store snacks.

The dog jumped up on the bed and snuggled next to her.

Clara sniffed the air. "Good grief," she said. "Now that I'm this close to you, I can smell you. You stink!" She put her unfinished cheese on the nightstand and picked up the dog. "I sure hope you don't have fleas!"

She took the dog into the bathroom and began running water into the tub. She tested and adjusted the water temperature twice. When the water was four inches deep, she lowered the dog into the water.

The dog didn't protest but stood impassive and obedient.

Clara used her hands to scoop water over the dog's back, then reached for her expensive salon shampoo. "Don't get used to this," she told her. "This is only because I don't have anything else to use."

She lathered and rinsed the compliant dog, changed the water in the tub, and repeated the process. Clara lifted the clean, sweet-smelling pooch out onto the bathmat. She shook herself vigorously as Clara turned towards the fresh towels that housekeeping had left for her. There was one bath towel, one hand towel, and one washcloth. Clara paused for an instant, then reached for the bath towel. She'd cope with drying herself with a hand towel in the morning; this dog required the bigger towel.

Clara rubbed the dog vigorously until her wet fur was only damp. Her thick coat was soft and silky. Her ears and tail were brown, tipped in white. The rest of her was a creamy white, with a brown stripe down the middle of her back. "You're a very pretty girl, aren't you?" Clara murmured.

The dog's tail came alive, thumping the side of the tub.

Clara sat back on her heels, the long day catching up with her.

The dog yawned in the turn-yourself-inside-out way that only dogs can do.

"You, too?" Clara asked. She grasped the towel bar and pulled herself to her feet. She patted her leg and the dog followed her out of the bathroom.

Clara fished the plush toy out of the shopping bag and held it out to the dog. "Here—it's an early Christmas present."

The dog took it gently between her teeth and swished her tail back and forth, keeping her eyes on Clara.

Clara slid out of her jeans and sweater and tossed them onto a chair. She turned back the covers and settled between the sheets.

The dog resumed her position next to Clara, her toy nestled next to her.

Clara extracted one arm from under the covers to cradle the dog. "Merry Christmas," she whispered as they both drifted off to sleep.

Chapter 18

Clara woke on Christmas morning to a small, warm mass plastered to her side. A soft, intermittent buzz came from the area by her knees. She reached out a hand and rested it lightly on the dog's side.

Her tail began to move, tickling Clara's nose. She chuckled and leaned forward, swiveling the dog carefully one hundred eighty degrees. "If you're going to be up here with me, I want to snuggle the other end."

The dog swiped her tongue over Clara's face and settled back down.

Clara buried her nose in the dog's neck, inhaling deeply the comforting scent of warm dog. "Do you want to go out?"

The dog didn't move.

"Tell you what," Clara said, throwing back the covers. "Let me get my clothes on, and we'll go to the diner to do your business. We'll come back here for your breakfast, and I'll shower and get ready. We'll go into town to see if we can find something for me to eat and somewhere to buy a bottle of wine to take when we go to Josef and Maisie's for dinner."

The dog lifted her head off of her paws and wagged her tail.

"Good!" Clara clipped the leash onto the collar, tucked the dog under her jacket, and opened the door to her room. A thick blanket of frost covered the ground and sparkled like yards of sequins in the brilliant sunshine.

Clara walked quickly to the now-familiar grassy spot and put the dog on the ground. Clara tilted her head to the sky and savored the feel of the sun on her face. For the first time in a very long time, Clara realized she was truly happy.

The dog finished her business, and they retraced their steps. Clara refilled the lid with water and placed more kibble on the towel, making a mental note to ask Maisie if she could borrow a couple of old bowls. "Give me fifteen," she said to the dog as she turned on the taps to the shower.

Refreshed and invigorated, Clara and the dog headed out. She knew she could go back to the convenience store they'd visited the night before, but she had plenty of time before she had to be at Josef and Maisie's for Christmas dinner, and she hadn't seen much of Pinewood during her month-long stay. Clara pulled up a map of the town on her phone and headed toward the downtown area. She'd surely find what she needed there.

The center of town was composed of one-way streets, two sets running east and west and two sets running north and south. She drove slowly up and down, keeping her eyes peeled for a market. On her second east-west pass, she found what she was looking for.

A cheery red and white sign in the window proclaimed that the establishment was, "Always Open." A placard over the door read, "Pinewood General Store. Est. 1898."

Clara parallel parked and turned to the dog who was sitting in the passenger seat, making a doggy-nose mess on the window. "You can't come in with me. Be a good girl, and I'll be as fast as I can."

She walked to the door, glancing at the window display as she passed by. Candy canes dressed in street clothes, arranged in a winter tableau depicting skaters on a pond and shoppers laden with packages, created a charming—albeit homemade—vignette. She would have loved to stop and examine it but remembered the dog and pushed on.

A rosy-cheeked young man greeted her with a hearty, "Merry Christmas."

In response to her question, he directed her to the well-stocked wine section and helped her make a selection.

When she asked about breakfast items, he led her to a small rack that contained individually packaged mass-market pastries.

Clara selected a small sleeve of powdered sugar donuts and followed the young man to the register.

"Would you like a cup of coffee to go with those?" he asked. "It's good. We grind our own beans."

"Sure."

"What'll you have?"

"Just black, thanks."

He swiveled to the elaborate coffee machine behind him and dispensed steaming liquid into a heavy paper cup. "This is on the house," he said, holding it out to Clara.

"Thank you. That's very nice of you," Clara replied, handing him cash for her wine and donuts and placing her change in the tip jar on the counter.

"That's an unusual display in your window," Clara said. "Charming."

"Thank you. My family's owned this general store for generations. We've been doing 'candy cane Christmas' since way before my mother was born. It's a legend around here."

"Deservedly so. Merry Christmas," she said as she turned to leave.

She got back in the car, set her coffee in the cup holder, and tore open the cellophane packaging of the donuts. She polished them off in record time, tearing off chunks to share with the dog as she ate. When she'd finished, she sipped her coffee and looked at the scene in front of her. Pinewood had an enticing downtown.

Clara took another sip, then turned to the dog. "Would you like to go for a walk? Let's take a good look at candy cane Christmas, then go exploring? What do you say?"

The dog's tail thumped the seat.

Clara finished her coffee and she and the dog set out. The dog stayed at her left side and sat patiently while she examined the display window.

When Clara turned and began walking down the street in the opposite direction, the dog kept pace and didn't tug or pull on the leash.

They came to the end of the block and paused while Clara considered which way to go. If she crossed the street and continued on, she'd be in the middle of a residential neighborhood. Handsome brick homes sat back from the street under canopies of mature trees that would be lush and green in springtime.

To her right was another row of storefronts. She loved to window-shop, so Clara headed that way.

The first store was a men's fine clothing boutique. The window display sported a mannequin dressed in a clean-lined tux, standing next to an antique table where a silver tray bearing two champagne flutes sat. A gift shop showcased an elegantly trimmed Christmas tree surrounded by carved nutcrackers. She continued walking past an art gallery and a bicycle shop. Each was well maintained and featured an artistic display window. *These folks certainly know how to merchandise*, she thought. Business must be booming in Pinewood.

Clara came to a duplex at the end of the block. One side held a store boasting the best selection of vintage guitars in the state. The other storefront was vacant, with a large For Lease sign in the window.

She stopped and pressed her forehead into the glass, inspecting the interior. It was a large, airy space with ample light from the north-facing windows. The high ceilings contained a labyrinth of newly painted ductwork and piping. The flooring was traditional black-and-white checkerboard. She could picture bakery cases lining the back and sides, with red tables and chairs filling the center space. The only thing she'd want to add would be retro pendant lights.

Clara first realized that she wasn't alone when the dog started wagging her tail. She swung around to face Kurt.

He opened his eyes wide. "I thought that was you, but the dog? Did you … get a dog?"

Clara grinned. "She's a stray. Long story."

Kurt arched an eyebrow. "If it's a stray, I'll bet that story has something to do with Josef?"

"Indeed," Clara laughed. "I offered to drop her at the shelter last night, but I got held up at the bakery and was too late to turn her in."

He squatted to pet the dog, who leapt up to kiss his face, then sat and accepted his attention politely.

"We've been hiding out in my motel room—where I'm not supposed to have dogs. It's such a nice day, I thought I'd take her for a walk and check out the town."

"This is a really nice collar and she's well cared for," he said. "Maybe she has an owner."

"I actually bought her that collar last night. And gave her a bath."

Kurt cut his eyes to hers.

"I needed the leash to take her over to the diner to relieve herself, so that no one at the motel saw me, and she was filthy, so I had to give her a bath. I didn't want her on the bed all dirty."

"She slept on the bed with you?" He stood, a grin playing at his lips.

Clara shrugged and pointed to the space behind her. "What used to be here, do you know?"

"It was a law firm."

"Why did it leave?"

"The solo practitioner joined a larger practice and moved into their offices."

"I see," Clara replied. She narrowed her eyes, staring into the empty storefront. "Any idea how much something like this rents for?"

"I know exactly how much," he replied. "Twelve fifty a month, plus utilities."

Clara's heart fluttered. A small bakery could generate enough revenue to be profitable at that rental cost. "Does this area get much foot traffic? These shops are all very nice. Do they do well?"

"Yes. All of them have been in business in these locations for more than twenty years. None of them has ever been late with their rent in all of that time."

She cocked her head to one side. "How do you know that?"

"Because I own all of the properties from here to the corner. I'm the attorney who moved out of this space." He smiled at her. "Are you thinking of opening a business?"

"I … I guess I am." She closed her eyes and took a deep breath. "I've always wanted to own a bakery. I'm a good baker, and I'm passionate about it." She opened her eyes and her expression was serious. "What do you think? Could I make a go of it in Pinewood—in this shop?"

"I believe you could be very successful here," he replied. "Retail businesses are always tricky, but you clearly know what you're doing in the kitchen. You've already got a lot of buzz going from those Christmas cookies. From what I've heard from Josef, you're an extremely hard worker. There's no reason you couldn't make a go of it." He grinned rakishly. "And I'm not just saying that because I'm a landlord with a space to rent."

Clara clasped her hands together. "How do we proceed? Do you have an application? Do you want to see my financials?"

Kurt took a business card out of his pocket and handed it to her. "Why don't you come see me tomorrow afternoon? About two. We can fill out all the paperwork then."

She pressed the card to her chest. "There's one more thing. Josef and Maisie have been so kind to me. In fact, I'm going there for Christmas dinner. Do you think they'll be upset? I'd be setting up a competing business. I won't do this if it will hurt them. I'll be on my way and find another town … "

"I know for a fact," Kurt cut her off, "that they would be delighted. I talked to Josef last night. He's worried about Maisie. They're going to cut way down on the baked goods they make for the diner."

"Oh, no," Clara said. "I'm sure that's very upsetting to her. They both take great pride in everything being homemade."

"He said that they'd disagreed about it—which is something they rarely do. He said he's going to insist." Kurt looked into Clara's eyes. "If you open a bakery, I'll bet they'll order what they need for the diner from you. Their account would set you up for success from the beginning. And it would certainly make Maisie and Josef feel like they aren't letting standards slip at the diner."

"Gosh," Clara said, raking her hand through her hair. "This is all working out perfectly. Like a Christmas miracle! Do you think I should mention it to them at dinner today?"

"We could mention it."

"You're going to be there? They didn't tell me."

"I'm with them every year." He cocked his head to one side. "Why don't we go together? I'll pick up both of you at three."

Clara nodded slowly, a smile spreading from her heart to her lips. "Perfect. You can help me work out what to say to them."

"I have a feeling that your decision to settle in Pinewood will be the best Christmas gift for them."

The dog, growing impatient at their feet, let out a short bark.

Kurt looked down at the dog, who was staring lovingly at Clara. "Now all you have to do is name your new dog."

Clara knelt beside her and hugged the dog. "Noelle," she said. "I think we're going to call you Noelle."

Noelle leapt to her feet and showered Clara with kisses.

Kurt reached out his hand to Clara.

She took it and he pulled her to her feet. "Welcome to Pinewood, Clara Conway—and Noelle. I think this is going to be the start of a wonderful new chapter … for all of us."

THE END

Thank You for Reading!

If you enjoyed *Paws & Pastries*,

I'd be grateful if you wrote a review.

Just a few lines would be great. Reviews are the best gift an author can receive. They encourage us when they're good, help us improve our next book when they're not, and help other readers make informed choices when purchasing books. Reviews keep the Amazon algorithms humming and are the most helpful aide in selling books! Thank you.

To post a review on Amazon:

1. Go to the product detail page for *Paws & Pastries* on Amazon.com.
2. Click "Write a customer review" in the Customer Reviews section.
3. Write your review and click Submit.

In gratitude,
Barbara Hinske

Acknowledgements

I'm blessed with the wisdom and support of many kind and generous people. I want to thank the most supportive and delightful group of champions an author could hope for:

My insightful and supportive assistant Lisa Coleman who offers exceptional editorial advice and keeps all the plates spinning;

My life coach Mat Boggs for your wisdom and guidance;

My kind and generous legal team, Kenneth Kleinberg, Esq., and Michael McCarthy—thank you for believing in my vision;

The professional "dream team" of my editor Jesika St. Clair and proofreader Dana Lee;

Elizabeth Mackey for a beautiful cover.

About the Author

BARBARA HINSKE recently left the practice of law to pursue her writing career full time. Her novella *The Christmas Club* has been made into a Hallmark Channel Christmas movie of the same name (2019), and she feels like she's living the dream. She is extremely grateful to her readers! She inherited the writing gene from her father who wrote mysteries when he retired and told her a story every night of her childhood. She and her husband share their own Rosemont with two adorable and spoiled dogs. The old house keeps her husband busy with repair projects and her happily decorating, entertaining, and gardening. She also spends a lot of time baking and—as a result—dieting.

Please enjoy this excerpt from Guiding Emily, the first book in the Emily series by Barbara Hinske:

Prologue

Emily. The woman who would become everything to me. The person I would eat every meal with and lie down next to every night—for the rest of my days.

She was just ahead; behind that door at the far end of the long hall. I glanced over my shoulder. Mark kept pace, slightly behind me. I could feel his excitement. It matched my own.

Everyone said Emily and I would be perfect for each other. I'd overheard them talking when they thought I was asleep. I spend a lot of time with my eyes closed, but I don't sleep much. They didn't know that.

"A magical match," they'd all agreed.

I lifted my eyes to Mark, and he nodded his encouragement. I gave a brief shake of my head. Only four more doorways between Emily and me.

I picked up my pace. A cylindrical orange object on the carpet in the third doorway from the end caught my eye. *Is that a Cheeto? A Crunchy Cheeto? I love Crunchy Cheetos.*

I tore my eyes away.

This was no time to get distracted.

We sped across the remaining distance to the doorway at the end of the hall. The door that separated me from my destiny.

I froze and waited while Mark knocked.

I heard Emily's voice—the sound I would come to love above all others—say, "Come in."

What was that in her voice? Eagerness—anxiety—maybe even a touch of fear? I'd take care of all of that right away.

The door swung open and Mark stepped back. He pointed to Emily.

I'd seen her before. Emily Main was a beautiful young woman in her late twenties. Auburn hair cascaded around her shoulders and shone like a new penny. With my jet-black coloring, we'd make a striking couple.

"Go on," Mark said.

I abandoned all my training—all sense of decorum—and raced to her.

Emily reached for me and flung her arms around my neck.

I placed my nose against her throat, and she tumbled out of her chair onto her knees.

I swept my tongue over her cheek, tasting the saltiness of her tears.

"Oh … Garth." My name on her lips came out in a hoarse whisper.

I wagged my tail so hard that we both lay back on the floor.

"Good boy, Garth!"

She rubbed the ridge of my skull behind my ears in a way that would become one of my favorite things in the whole wide world.

Next to food.

Especially Crunchy Cheetos.

Mark and the other trainers were right—we were made for each other. I was the perfect guide dog for Emily Main.

Chapter 1

"Weren't you supposed to leave for the airport half an hour ago?" Michael Ward asked his boss, whose fingers were typing furiously on her keyboard. "You're still planning to get married, aren't you?"

Emily Main's head bobbed behind the computer, her eyes fixed to the screen.

"I can't believe you put off a departure to Fiji to help us launch this new program. Your wedding's in two days."

"We've been working on this for almost a year. I wasn't about to leave when we're this close. I just need to finish this last email." She hunched forward and peered at the computer screen.

"There," she said, pushing her office chair back as the email *whooshed* from her inbox. "Done."

She looked up at Michael, blinking. It was probably the first time she had looked at anything besides a computer screen in hours. "I brought my suitcase so I could go to the airport straight from the office. I don't have to stop at home."

Michael raised his eyebrows at her. "That's all you've got? A carry-on and a satchel for a week—a week that includes your wedding? My wife packs more than that for a three-day weekend."

"My wedding dress is a classic sheath and the rest is bathing suits and shorts."

"I would have thought Connor Harrington the third would have wanted an elaborate wedding—one fit for the society pages."

"Our wedding is going to be very elegant—think JFK Junior and Carolyn," Emily said, flinging her purse over her shoulder and reaching for the retractable handle of her suitcase.

Michael stepped in front of her. "I've got this," he said. "I'll walk you to the street. I'd like to congratulate Connor on snagging our office hero."

Emily hesitated.

"He is picking you up, isn't he? You're flying there together?"

"He went out over the weekend. He wanted to do some diving with his best man … sort of a bachelor party reprise. I was traveling with my mom and maid of honor, but they flew out yesterday as planned. The company paid to change my ticket, but it would have cost almost five hundred dollars for Mom and Gina to change theirs. It wasn't worth it."

"But you don't like to fly." He peered into Emily's face. "Did you talk to Connor about that before you decided to stay an extra day? You have told him about your fear of flying, haven't you?"

Emily shrugged. "I've mentioned it, sure, but I haven't made a big deal out of it."

"So what did he say?"

"He suggested that I get a prescription for Xanax and sleep the whole way out there."

"Really? That's what he said?"

"He's a Brit, for heaven's sake. 'Stiff upper lip' and all that. He's not the sort of guy to coddle anyone—and I'm not a needy type of gal. You know that."

Michael cocked his head to one side. "Do you have to change planes?"

Emily nodded.

"You don't want to be knocked out for that."

"I'll be fine." Emily threw her shoulders back. "You don't need to worry about me."

"I know—I'm sorry. It's just that I wouldn't let my wife make the trip alone if she felt like you do about flying."

"I fly alone all the time, and nothing's ever happened to me. There's no reason this time should be any different."

Michael lifted his hands, palms facing her, and shrugged. "Okay, but I think he could have at least offered to pay to change your mom's flight or something."

"I'll be perfectly fine." Emily walked past him into the hallway. "I promised Dhruv that I'd say goodbye before I leave."

"He's going to miss you. You're the one person here that really connects with him."

Michael watched her shoulders sag slightly.

"Hey," he said, rolling the carry-on to a halt beside her in the hall. "I'm sorry. I didn't mean to worry you. The whole team is going to step into your shoes while you're gone. We've talked about it."

"Of course you will. I shouldn't worry about him. I've got the best team in San Francisco. Scratch that. On the entire West Coast." Emily gave him a teary smile and punched him playfully on the shoulder. "I know you'll take care of everything while I'm away, Michael—including helping Dhruv stay connected with the team."

"Good!" Michael continued down the hallway. "I don't want you to give this place a second thought while you're gone. If anyone deserves a vacation—and a gorgeous beach wedding—it's you, Em. But don't get too comfortable." Michael turned and smiled at her. "We do need you to come back. We'd be lost without you here."

Emily laughed and pushed him toward the elevator. "Why don't you go push that button, you wonderful suck-up. It'll take ages to get an elevator this time of the morning. I'll stick my head into Dhruv's cubicle and be right back."

Emily found Dhruv, as usual, leaning into the bank of computer monitors, intently focused on the complex strings of code in front of him. She cleared her throat. When Dhruv didn't move, she tapped him lightly on the shoulder.

Dhruv sat back quickly and spun around. A smile spread across his face when he saw her.

"I wanted to say goodbye before I go."

Dhruv nodded. "Goodbye."

"I'll see you a week from Monday."

"I know. You're getting married in two days, then you have your honeymoon for a week, then you come back to work," he recited.

"That's right. You remembered."

"I remember things."

"Yes, you do. That's one reason you're so very good at programming," she said.

"I know."

"Okay … well … have a good week. You can go to Michael if you have … if you need anything."

"I know."

Emily regarded the shy, socially awkward middle-aged man who was, by far, the most proficient member of her extremely talented team of programmers. "Bye."

Dhruv nodded.

Emily stepped away.

Dhruv leapt out of his chair and called after her. "Have a happy wedding."

Emily swung around and gave him a thumbs-up then turned back toward the elevators where Michael was waiting.

Available at Amazon in Print, Audio, and for Kindle

Novels in the Rosemont Series

Coming to Rosemont

Weaving the Strands

Uncovering Secrets

Drawing Close

Bringing Them Home

Shelving Doubts

Restoring What Was Lost

Novellas

The Night Train

The Christmas Club (adapted for The Hallmark Channel, 2019)

Paws & Pastries

Novels in the Emily Series

Guiding Emily

Novels in the "Who's There?!" Collection

DEADLY PARCEL

FINAL CIRCUIT

I'd Love to Hear from You! Connect with Me Online:

Sign up for my newsletter at
BarbaraHinske.com to receive your Free Gift,
plus Inside Scoops and Bedtime Stories.

Search for **Barbara Hinske on YouTube**
for tours inside my own historic home plus tips
and tricks for busy women!

Find photos of fictional Rosemont and Westbury,
adorable dogs, and things related to her books at
Pinterest.com/BarbaraHinske.

Email me at **bhinske@gmail.com** or find me at
Instagram/barbarahinskeauthor
Facebook.com/BHinske
Twitter.com/BarbaraHinske

CPSIA information can be obtained
at www.ICGtesting.com
Printed in the USA
BVHW071536071220
595086BV00007B/1001

9 781734 924923